THE COLDEST WAR

AN ATTICUS WOLFE NOVEL

DAVE SINCLAIR

Time has run out for Atticus Wolfe.

October 1964

The two most formidable superpowers the world has ever seen are on the precipice of all-out nuclear war; and it's all Atticus Wolfe's fault.

A twenty-first century spy trapped in the swinging sixties, Atticus has a lot on his plate.

While the Soviet Union and the USA prepare for an unthinkable war, Atticus must face the man responsible for swerving history from its path into all-out annihilation.

And that's not all he has to deal with.

How do you fight a war when you can't even trust yourself? With every corrective action pushing the world closer to the brink, Atticus must work with friends and enemies alike to stave off Armageddon.

With mind-bending twists, *The Coldest War* is a page burner of an espionage thriller unlike any you've read before.

ALSO BY DAVE SINCLAIR

Atticus Wolfe Novels

Out of Time

It Takes a Spy

The Coldest War

Charles Bishop Novels

Kiss My Assassin

Agent Provocateur

Venetian Blonde

Eva Destruction Novels

The Barista's Guide to Espionage

The Rookie's Guide to Espionage (novella)

The Amnesiac's Guide to Espionage

The Dead Spy's Guide to Espionage

For Esther.
Keep shining that light everywhere you go.
Love you more than Barbecue Shapes.

PROLOGUE

I t wasn't the first time Omar Ganim had had a gun pointed at his face.

But given the unhinged nature of the person wielding the weapon, he suspected it would be the last.

Ganim had broken into Atticus Wolfe's flat and made himself at home, patiently awaiting the MI6 spy's return. But it wasn't Wolfe who crashed through the front door in a disturbed frenzy. It was someone else entirely.

The newcomer bounded into the airy loft brandishing a pistol, his crazed eyes ablaze. Looking like a rain-drenched rat, he scanned the room, eyes passing over Ganim like a raging river over a rock. Only when the manic man had determined that the object of his wrath wasn't present did he turn his attention to Ganim.

Voice calm and level, Ganim addressed the wide-eyed bespectacled man before him. "I don't believe we've had the pleasure."

Seemingly surprised the other party possessed the ability to speak, it took a moment before he was calm enough to talk. "Who're you?"

"I could ask you the same thing, friend. You're the one who kicked down the door."

The man nodded, circled the room in a daze, panting. Stopping suddenly, he rubbed the side of his head with the barrel of his pistol.

Ganim did his best to sound sympathetic. "You seem... distracted. Are you alright?"

The soaking man glanced vaguely in his direction. "Have you ever been in love?" Staring at Ganim directly now, he leaned forward. "I mean *really* in love. Your heart, your soul, everything invested in another human being in a way you never thought possible?"

The man was most certainly not alright. His mental state seemed to be dissolving by the second. He pointed his gun at Ganim to remind him that a question had been asked. Sensing a non-answer would be unacceptable, Ganim answered truthfully.

"Once. It was during the Weimar Republic, between the wars. Germans had lost their collective minds. Free-flowing booze and cocaine, you name it. Free love before everyone thinks it's going to be invented, debauchery and hedonism the likes of which hadn't been seen since the Romans. She brought out the best in me, even saw the worst and helped me hold it in check. She was a manifestation of life itself. A whirlwind, a force of nature. Far better than this world deserved." Ganim realised he was rambling, but Ilse was the one subject on which he found it impossible to hold back. The emotions were too great. "I was all set to marry her, you know, before she came to her senses. Nine days before the wedding we were meant to meet on Unter den Linden, a boulevard whose name literally means 'under the linden trees'. I was running late, as usual. Before I got there a car, a

Horch, came hurtling down the road. A little girl with pigtails crossed without looking." Ganim's voice hitched. "Ilse didn't even hesitate. She ran out and pushed the girl out of the way. The doctor said she didn't die straight away. She lost her life lying on the road, in agony, alone. So, yes, I do know something about love. I know all about loss, too. Every partner I had since understood they were competing with a ghost. They all gave up trying eventually."

The drenched man bowed his head sagely. "The only person who ever saw you?"

"Yes, exactly that." Ganim gulped. The next part was a gamble. "You've lost someone like that, recently?"

"Yes." His eyes glazed over, unfocused.

"Oh, I'm so sorry. She must have been a hell of a woman."

"He was."

Seemingly at a loss as to what to do next, the man flopped into the armchair opposite Ganim with a squelch. He tilted his head inquisitively and said, "You ever have one of those days you just wish you could reverse time?"

"Constantly."

Distracted, the man watched water flowing down his tilted palm. As if belatedly remembering he was taking part in a conversation, he turned to Ganim, eyes glazed over. "Going to be invented."

"What's that?"

"Free love before everyone thinks it's going to be invented. That's what you said, word for word. I have a mind for detail." His eyes narrowed. "Atticus Wolfe uses phrases like that. Acts Like he's so much smarter than everyone else because he thinks he knows how history is going to unfold." The man's face turned hard, his jaw set.

"Who are you, old man?" He raised the pistol. "Wolfe doesn't have friends."

The rain outside grew heavier. Ganim was unsure if it was the clouds or the company that made the room darker.

The man leant forward ominously. "I won't ask again."

"Omar."

"Your *last* name?"

"Ganim."

The other man recoiled in shock. He stood, eyes once again wild and unhinged. "Ganim! You're the one who sent Wolfe back in time!"

"Not by choice. He kind of hitched an impromptu ride. Believe me, it was not my intent. He was chasing me, and—"

"You're old. Why are you old?"

"I was sent back a little farther than Atticus's sixty odd years. I've been here a long time."

The man's eyes narrowed. "Wolfe killed my lover."

"Oh. I see."

"I came here to kill him but found you instead." The pistol danced in his hands. "You're friends with that murderer now? Is that why you're here?"

"I wouldn't say friends, no." Ganim smoothed down his trousers, which needed no smoothing. "Grudging acquaintances? Reluctant associates? Distant and separate colleagues." Seeing the mounting anger gripping the other man, he added, "Very distant." Ganim could see the wheels turning in the man's mind, just as they were in his own. "You're the double agent chap. Oliver something. The one who wants to change history. I thought you were safely tucked away behind the Iron Curtain." Oliver Something stepped forward and forcibly pressed the gun into Ganim's forehead. "Obviously not," he added.

"What are you doing in Wolfe's flat as a very distant colleague?"

"We occasionally get together and talk about old times."

Oliver inhaled unsteadily. "You're lying." He tilted his head and his eyes drilled into Ganim's soul. "Why would the man who invented the time machine that brought you both here hang out with the MI6 agent who was hunting him down?" He exhaled slowly. "You wouldn't be planning a way to get back home, would you? The two of you plotting to pop back to the good old twenty-first century when no one is looking?"

Ganim had never been particularly good at card games. It had been said his poker face was akin to a three-year-old with a secret.

It was plain Oliver's mind was racing. Rubbing his chin with the barrel of his pistol, he paced about the flat, talking to himself. "A man from the future, no, a *scientist* from the future who knows about time travel; how events will unfold, who creates what technology." Oliver turned and issued a sinister chuckle. "I think you'll be a worthy addition to the great and glorious Soviet cause."

"Oh, I'd love to but I'm afraid I'm already late for Pilates."

Oliver aimed the gun at Ganim's chest. "I'm *afraid* I really must insist."

"There's a wonderfully elegant phrase they use in my time. It seems most apt at this juncture." Ganim pushed himself to his feet defiantly. "It really is a beautiful turn of phrase. It goes: get fucked, you wacked-out weirdo."

"Last chance." Oliver cocked the pistol. "Come willingly or—"

"What are you going to do? Shoot me?"

Oliver stepped back. "Well, as a matter of fact."

He fired. Ganim screamed in agony, clutching his side, and stumbled backwards into the chair. Blood flowed through his fingers. He couldn't stem the bleeding.

Fighting through the pain, he screeched, "What the hell? I'm no use to you dead!"

"You're not going to die, old man. You'll be patched up just fine. This is to shut you up more than anything, and to leave Wolfe a calling card. You're coming with me. We're going to achieve great things, Omar Ganim."

Ganim sucked air between his teeth, fighting the mounting nausea. "And what exactly are we going to achieve?"

Oliver's voice was triumphant. "I have these."

He delved into his coat pocket and extracted several black and white photographs. They were pictures of text. Ganim didn't know the book, but from the few scant pages he saw, it was clearly a history of the Cold War. A history yet to take place.

Oliver grinned. "You and I are going to change the world."

CHAPTER
ONE

T ime travel, it turns out, is complicated.

Atticus Wolfe stared at the man who had just, quite literally, materialised out of thin air in the middle of his flat. The other gentleman's name was also Atticus Wolfe.

Really complicated.

The newly arrived Atticus was dressed in the drab green military uniform of the Soviet army. He grabbed Atticus's glass of scotch, slugged it down and told them to listen closely—and then didn't utter a word. There was a swirling silence as Maggie and the two versions of her boyfriend stood awkwardly, a million questions hanging between them and, evidently, no clue where to start.

It was Maggie who finally articulated the sentiment that encapsulated the current disposition of all those assembled. "What the ever-living fuck is going on?"

Atticus thought it a fair question. He and Maggie had returned from a funeral, found the flat ransacked, complete with a blood-soaked chair and an ominous note. They naively thought that was the sum total of spectacle the day had in store for them. It's amazing how wrong two people can be.

The newly materialised Atticus held up a soothing hand. "I'm from the future. Your future, a year from now."

Atticus thought the older man's face seemed slightly off. It took him a few seconds to realise why. He'd always seen his face in reflection, whereas this man's face was flesh and blood before him.

Outwardly, Younger Atticus was doing his best to display a calm and rational exterior. Inside was a completely different story. In fact, the he would go so far as to say he was freaking out. *Another* Atticus was standing in front of him. He was having a calm and rational conversation *with himself*. This was on par with the time he went to South America, took ayahuasca and tripped balls so much he had a casual chat with God. Except this time there were no hallucinogens involved.

Doing his best impersonation of a composed human being, Younger Atticus asked, "How are things, a year from now?"

The older Atticus gave his counterpart a humourless smile. "I wouldn't be here if things weren't bad."

"Define bad."

"Really bad."

Younger Atticus grunted. "Really is an adverb, not a description."

Maggie elbowed Younger Atticus. "Are you correcting your own grammar?"

She appeared to be handling events better than he was.

Younger Atticus smirked. "Seems like it, but old Atticus here—"

"Who're you calling old?"

"—is being evasive and I want to know why."

Older Atticus tugged at his military jacket. "Because I don't want to mess up the timeline any more than I already have. Than *we* already have."

Younger Atticus scratched his stubbled chin. He wasn't in the right mindset for this kind of discussion. He doubted he ever would be. "Have we had this conversation before?"

"What? As in, have I been here before, talking to you, me?" Older squinted. "Have I had this conversation before, when you were me where I am, uh, now?"

Both Atticuses rubbed their left temple at the same time. It seemed they both had the same opinion on time travel discussions.

Older Atticus went on. "No. We haven't had this conversation. I never was where you are now. This is new for me too. Desperation led me to come here, to try and fix things."

"Desperation? How bad do things get? There's *more* disruption to history?"

Atticus had already disturbed the timeline plenty since he'd arrived in the sixties from the 2020s. Uncovering a mole in MI6 that would have likely stayed concealed, preventing a life-defining injury to his father, not to mention the explosion that killed twenty-seven members of MI6 who would have remained unharmed if Atticus had stayed in his own time. He wouldn't have thought the situation could become much graver.

Older Atticus's expression was measured. "You could say things have gotten worse."

"That's just fucking vague. Stop with the Obi-Wan Kenobi bullshit and give us some specifics."

The fact that Atticus was—literally—arguing with himself was bending his mind. Not only was his slightly older self being evasive, he had to know his answers were

9

infuriating. Yet here he was, deliberately baiting himself. For a moment Atticus felt an immense sympathy for all those he'd interrogated over the years. He could be a right asshole.

Young Atticus inhaled deeply. "Give me something tangible. How bad is it?"

"You know Saigon?"

"I'm familiar with it." Except in Atticus's time—well, both their time—it was known as Ho Chi Minh City, renamed after the fall of Saigon at the end of the Vietnam War. "What about it?"

"It's not there anymore." Atticus's face was ashen, like the blood of millions were on his hands. There was a reason for that.

"How?"

"You know how. The history books Oliver stole from my phone, your phone—*our* phone. He tried to manipulate how the twentieth century panned out. He succeeded in changing things, but certainly not for the better."

Older Atticus told the tale of escalation. He first realised history was amiss when Leonid Brezhnev come to power in late 1964, only to be toppled months later. Brezhnev should have been Soviet leader for decades. History knew him as a conservative and pragmatic party man who brought a level-headedness to the Cold War and went on to deescalate the mounting tensions of the time.

His tenure as General Secretary was also known for its inefficiency, corruption, economic stagnation and inability to close the mounting technological divide with the West. He eventually paved the way for Mikhail Gorbachev with his glasnost and perestroika policies, which ultimately dismantled the Soviet regime. He paved the way for the Cold War to deescalate and ultimately end. The failure of

Brezhnev to come to power could only have come about because of one man within the Soviet Union. And again, it was Atticus's fault.

Older Atticus told them Alexander Nikolayevich Shelepin had become Soviet leader after Brezhnev suffered a series of scandals and political setbacks. As neither of these things had happened in Atticus's history, there was only one explanation.

Shelepin was the former head of the KGB and was a hard-line opponent of détente with the West. As with all freshly crowned leaders, Shelepin ached for an opportunity to flex his newly acquired muscles. He bit off more than he could chew with Vietnam, and the situation steadily grew out of hand.

Still smarting after their humiliating backdown in Cuba in 1962, there were vocal sections of the Soviet party who believed they had capitulated too much to the West; Shelepin among them. The Americans, under the leadership of Johnson, had escalated the conformation in Vietnam, significantly increasing their bombing in the north. Under Shelepin's stewardship, the Soviet Union did far more than supply moral, logistic and military support to North Vietnam; they became actively involved, kicking off a direct Cold War confrontation that had not occurred in Atticus's past.

The history Atticus knew was no more.

There was only one way Shelepin could have become General Secretary: Oliver. He must have manipulated events to put his puppet in place instead of Brezhnev. The man who had Atticus's history book was rewriting it, and destroying the world in the process. If Younger Atticus needed proof Oliver Preston was the most dangerous man on the planet, Older Atticus had just supplied it.

"The situation quickly grew uncontrollable on both sides. No one knew how to contain it. It escalated by the day. The south would bomb the north. The next day the north would retaliate double, and the south would reciprocate in kind. Everyone saw it coming, yet no one could stop it. The better part of two million people were wiped out in an instant. The world's still reeling, but the retaliation has already begun."

Atticus recognised the tone, *his* tone, and suspected there was far more that remained unsaid. The man before him was defeated, overwhelmed with the earth-shattering events that, while not directly of his making, would never have occurred if he hadn't fallen through time.

"That's why you're here?"

"That's why I'm here."

Younger Atticus lowered his gaze. "Because you screwed everything up."

"Listen..."

"You fucked everything up so monumentally that millions died. Because of you."

Older Atticus clenched his fists. Maggie placed a hand on Younger Atticus's arm in an attempt to quell his rising anger.

The older version of himself clenched his jaw. "*We* fucked up. *We* screwed up the timeline! *Our* presence, *our* mere existence here caused the world to become completely screwed. I'm not the bad guy. I've come to you to fix it. I sacrificed... everything... to come here. You're me, dickhead, so don't try and take the moral high ground."

"What I think he meant to say," Maggie's soothing voice interrupted the mounting tension, "was that we appreciate you coming to help us fix this."

Maggie's eyes flared at the Younger Atticus, and he

couldn't help but smirk at her sage interruption. He found it amusing that out of those in the room, she was the one who knew him the best.

Taking a big breath, Younger Atticus held up a conciliatory hand. He inhaled, giving them all a moment to calm down. "I assume you have a plan to stop it from happening?"

Older Atticus's mood shifted slightly. There was a twinkle in his eye. "Have you met me?"

"Before today, no."

"Yeah, okay, that's fair." His older self rubbed the back of his neck. "I, uh. Right, this is weird for everyone."

"See how no one is arguing with you?" Maggie seemed as perplexed as Younger Atticus, but with a semi-amused smirk.

In the six months Younger Atticus had known Maggie, she'd been though a lot. The rogue Mod within MI6 had been catapulted from secretary to field agent, found out her best friend was a Soviet spy, discovered she was working with a man from the future and eventually fell in love with him. The rate of change for Maggie must have been the reason she accepted this additional Atticus in their midst so calmly.

Checking her nails, Maggie didn't look up as she asked, "What happened to me? To everyone at MI6, to—"

Older Atticus held up a hand. "I can't tell you. I'm sorry."

He appeared genuinely upset. Atticus detected a palpable melancholy in his older self.

Older Atticus went on. "I'm sure you understand, this is all very delicate. Telling you or anyone too much risks everything we're trying to prevent. I'm only revealing enough to ensure you understand the urgency."

"So, we have to just trust you?"

Older Atticus smiled. "Is there someone else you trust more than yourself?" The other Atticus waited for the pause to hit home, then added, "Because I can tell you, you don't. And I should know."

For several moments the three of them seemed unsure what to say next. The peculiarity of the situation was manifest in every half-glimpse and awkward commencement of sentences that went unfinished.

Maggie slapped her hands together and surprised the Atticuses. "So, let's have it. What's the tactical officer's play to undo a nuclear holocaust?"

Older Atticus asked them to sit. Over the next half hour, he laid out his plan in detail. It would be fair to categorise the ensuing silence that followed as stunned.

Eventually, Younger Atticus spoke. "Rathdowne's going to love this."

"No, he won't." Older Atticus smiled. "He didn't in my time, even after Saigon went radioactive. But really, by then it was too late. I can't imagine your Rathdowne will be more receptive."

"How did you get here? The time travel, I mean." Atticus had so many questions he wanted to write a list.

"Look, I'm not going to get into that just yet."

"What about the Red Army uniform?" Maggie eyed him pointedly from head to toe. "Not exactly something one picks up on Savile Row. Any comment on that?"

"Not at this time, no." Older Atticus folded his hands in front of him.

Younger Atticus raised an eyebrow. "Would you accept those answers?"

"No."

"But you expect me to?"

"I do." Older Atticus left it at that.

Younger Atticus turned to Maggie. "Am I always this evasive?"

"Honestly?" A smirk creased the corner of her mouth. "Pretty often. Annoying, isn't it?"

Older Atticus stepped in before they could become sidetracked. "I'm giving you all you need to know at this stage, the bare minimum." His shoulders relaxed. "I realise that's a shit answer, but I can't risk giving you too much information. Anything else might change things even more. Christ knows I've—*we've*—fucked up the timeline enough. If I tell you too much, events that should have occurred might not happen, or the bad things I've seen could become even worse."

Both Atticuses rubbed their left temples again.

"Right." Younger Atticus sighed. There was a hell of a lot to take in, even though his older self was giving only half answers. "We all need some time to process this."

"And a drink." Maggie waved her empty glass. "Definitely more drinks."

Both Atticuses nodded. Maggie did the honours.

Mind racing ahead twelve steps, Younger Atticus asked, "I assume you'll need to crash here?"

Older Atticus shrugged. "It's not like I had time to book an Airbnb."

Maggie scrunched her face into an *I don't get it* expression. Both Atticuses laughed.

More drinks were poured and the mood relaxed. Atticus still couldn't believe another him was sitting in this room, telling Maggie *his* stories. It was surreal in the most precise dictionary meaning of the word.

Older Atticus was clearly as ill at ease as he was. It was odd for all three of them. There was a sadness in the other Atticus too, though he refused to discuss why.

As peculiar as it was having another Atticus there, Younger Atticus found it wasn't as strange as it could have been. It wasn't like they had to spend time getting to know him; they already knew him intimately. This casual acceptance of another version of himself should have made the whole idea even more bizarre.

The more the drinks flowed, the more the atmosphere in the room lightened. They even laughed together. There were shared jokes, which made sense, actually. They all had the same cultural references and experiences, in all sorts of ways.

After they finished the bottle, Maggie swayed towards the kitchen and returned with another. Her words were clear, if slightly slurred.

"I'm just going to come out and address the elephant in the room."

Both Atticuses turned to her, curious.

"There's one of me and two of you."

"Yes?" Younger Atticus couldn't fault her math.

She coyly swivelled her shoulders. "I'm okay with that, in case anyone was asking."

"Okay with..." Younger Atticus said, confused. And then, "Oh."

Older Atticus added, "Oh."

"Yeah." The most wicked grin crossed Maggie's crimson lips. "I'm really okay with that. I'm not saying right now, and maybe it's the booze talking, but maybe it's a thing that could happen one day?" She hefted a quizzical eyebrow.

"I mean, it's technically not cheating, is it?" Younger Atticus frowned. "Is it?"

Older Atticus scratched the back of his bald head. "I guess it's not, no."

"But not now?" Older Atticus asked.

"No, of course not." Younger Atticus sounded as unsure as his counterpart.

"No," Maggie added, issuing them awkward sideways glances, "obviously not now."

They agreed to drop the subject and they all slept poorly.

TWO

The displays may have been different, but the Natural History Museum had the same welcoming sense of awe. Not that it was called that yet. In this time, it was known as the British Museum (Natural History).

Atticus had selected a neutral venue for the meeting, and the grand Hintze Hall was certainly a striking choice. While he waited, Atticus took in his surrounds. Beside him was the skeleton of an African elephant known as George.

The glass cabinets and displays exhibited specimens from all corners of the globe, or—as it was still considered at this time—the great and glorious British Empire. Atticus didn't have the heart to reveal that the rest of the world didn't feel quite the same way about the Empire as the Empire did.

At precisely the stroke of nine am his meeting companion entered the great hall and made a beeline straight for him. He sat with a grunt.

"This is dramatic." Rathdowne regarded the high

ornate ceiling. "No one ever accused you of being subtle, Wolfe."

You have no idea. Atticus was almost looking forward to the next few minutes. Almost.

"I have a busy day, Wolfe, I'd appreciate you getting on with whatever it is you dragged me out here to discuss."

Atticus paused. "You don't like me very much, do you?"

Rathdowne's face turned a darker shade of red. It was hard to tell if he was annoyed because he'd been called to this meeting or if he was genuinely pissed off at Atticus. Atticus had always sensed Rathdowne disliked him, although it was hard to know if that was due to Atticus himself or because Rathdowne hated everyone.

Initially he'd thought it due to the colour of his skin—right up until his boss had decked another employee for casting a racial slur in Atticus's direction. Since learning Atticus was from the future, however, their relationship hadn't exactly thawed.

Rathdowne opened his mouth to speak, then seemed to think better of it. "I was going to say something diplomatic, like a manager is meant to, but the truth of the matter is, no, I don't like you, Wolfe." He smoothed down his moustache, taking a moment to steady himself. "I think you're a danger to national security. You're reckless, impulsive and, most infuriatingly, you're often right. Do you know how bloody annoying that is? How annoying *you* are? I work with you because I have to, because you're good at what you do, but I don't want to associate with you any more than I have to. The less time I spend with Atticus Wolfe, the better."

Atticus sucked air between his teeth. "One day you're going to look back at the timing of that statement and laugh." Atticus paused. "But I'm thinking it won't be today."

Over the next few minutes Atticus outlined how Oliver would divert the course of history, how he now possessed the history of the Cold War and knew the outcome of every decision the superpowers would make. Then he went on to explain that those events were no longer going to unfold, thanks to Oliver; that in the next few months the former MI6 employee would somehow instil Shelepin as General Secretary of the Soviet Union instead of the more conservative Brezhnev, with catastrophic consequences.

Rathdowne gave Atticus the evil eye and twitched like a bubble bath enthusiast hugging a toaster. Not finished, Atticus went on to explain that in less than a year the Cold War would escalate to hot. Millions would die. History would not just be altered, it would be irrevocably blown apart.

Atticus paused, giving Rathdowne a moment to process this information. One of Rathdowne's eyes had increased its twitching, and Atticus was reasonably sure he detected drool. It appeared the other man's brain was short circuiting. Atticus almost felt sorry for him, knowing what was about to transpire.

"And how the hell do you know any of this?" Rathdowne's voice lowered and raised like a rollercoaster. "About the future? This altered future?"

"I have a man who went through it all firsthand, and is willing to explain what happened."

"Is he reliable?"

"Depends who you ask."

He gave the signal, and from across the great hall two figures approached. One was familiar to Rathdowne; he'd seen Maggie the day before. The other figure was equally familiar, but far more alarming.

The other Atticus wore one of Younger Atticus's suits, which, unsurprisingly, fitted him too. Atticus was no closer to being comfortable in his other self's presence. Hell, would anyone be? The whole situation was bizarre. Older Atticus was overly affectionate with Maggie, which rankled Atticus, but he recognised he'd be the same with her were the situation reversed. Which, of course, it was.

Atticus felt a headache coming on just thinking about it.

They'd all agreed the Older Atticus should sleep on the couch, and he'd gone with some reluctance. The morning had been no less awkward. Occasionally they'd fall into moments of familiar routine only to suddenly pull themselves up, realising the utter weirdness of their situation.

It was plain that Maggie was just as confused as the two Atticuses. The Older Atticus wasn't an imposter, wasn't someone who looked similar to the man she loved, he *was* the man she loved. The real him, only a slightly different version. She did her best to stick close to *her* Atticus, staying true to the man who, as she put it, was here first. It was a confusing time for them all.

Seeing the two of them stride across the grand hall of the Natural History Museum, Atticus was again struck by pangs of unreasonable jealousy. He watched Maggie laugh at a snide joke Older Atticus made on their way over. Younger Atticus thought perhaps his jealousy wasn't completely unreasonable. In retrospect, he was grateful they hadn't taken up Maggie's opportune suggestion from the night before. The situation was complicated enough already.

The audible groan from Rathdowne brought Atticus's

attention back to the present. In retrospect, it was less a groan, more of a whimper.

After several failed attempts at conversing, Rathdowne finally regained the ability to speak. "Is this more Buck Rogers bullshit?"

"I'm afraid so."

Maggie and the other Atticus joined them and made the briefest of introductions. Rathdowne's eye twitch doubled down. In quick order, Younger Atticus explained the swirling time vortex that manifested itself in the middle of his flat and the man who had staggered out. Older Atticus took up the story and recounted what he'd told them the night before; he was from one year hence and the world had gone to hell. Oliver had made good on his promise to reshape history with devastating consequences.

Gulping, Rathdowne was struggling to come to terms with what he had been told. Saigon was no more and the superpowers were on the brink of war. Just like Younger Atticus and Maggie, it took a while.

"Just what the world needs," he massaged the sides of his head, "two bloody Atticus Wolfes."

"Now you can understand why we didn't want to meet in the office." Younger Atticus did his best to sound conciliatory. "Don't want to scare the natives."

Scanning the hall, Rathdowne kept his voice low. "People are noticing there's two of you."

"People have heard of twins before, Rathdowne." Older Atticus folded his arms. "It's not uncommon."

Rathdowne only grunted in response, and Atticus was sure his face grew even more red. Before the man exploded, he thought it best to outline what they had in mind.

"We have a plan—well, a sketch of a plan—to fix this thing. To stop Oliver. We'll need to talk to a few people to determine if it's viable, then we'll present it to you. I'm estimating three days. How does that sound?"

Sighing, Rathdowne glanced up at George the elephant. "I assume this plan you have in mind is one I'm not going to like in the slightest?"

Younger Atticus folded his hands in front of him and grinned.

"What does that smile mean?" Rathdowne's gaze darted between Maggie and Older Atticus. "I can't tell. Is that a good smile?"

Older Atticus and Maggie answered him in unison. "No."

Maggie and both Atticuses got to work on the plan in their new office at the Tower of London. It was generous to call the room they resided in an office, really. But what it lacked in the traditional office amenities it made up for in medieval opulence. The numerous suits of armour and feudal weaponry gave the room a distinct ambience.

After the last MI6 office had been blown up by one of Oliver's henchmen, MI6 had to improvise until a new headquarters could be sourced. As far as the general public was concerned, the Tower of London was temporarily closed, for the first time since World War Two. During that time, it had housed prisoners of war. Now it protected, rather than incarcerated.

Most of the White Tower building had been handed over to MI6 as emergency office space, although large portions of the overall fortress were designated no-go zones. Atticus had requested to be stationed in the Crown Jewels exhibit, but apparently that was deemed inappropriate. There were signs everywhere advising MI6 staff where they could and couldn't go. One might construe this as a sign that the Beefeaters didn't trust the Secret Intelligence Service to keep their hands off the Queen's valuables.

For three solid days and nights the small group laboured away on their plan. After the first day working together in the Tower, they had their entry and exit routine down. One Atticus would arrive early, then an hour later the other would arrive. Occasionally someone would shoot them a *didn't you already come in?* look, but no one had said anything yet. The three ensured their office was locked at all times, and whenever someone came by, Older Atticus had the pleasure of standing in the broom closet.

It wasn't an elegant solution, but it worked. The three toiled away at the finer points of the plan. The other Atticus seemed as determined and focused as his younger self. In fact, often more so. Having seen what was to come, he was particularly motivated to prevent that outcome from coming to fruition.

Their interactions flipped between awkward and completely natural. Sometimes Atticus felt like he was talking to himself, which was, of course, literally what he was doing.

Older Atticus stood over a rolled-out map of Soviet Russia that was spread across the wooden table. He had a pencil tucked behind his ear and a pad full of scribbled notes in his hand. Younger Atticus couldn't recall ever tucking pencils behind his ears. Was that a thing he did?

Older Atticus pointed to central Siberia. "If the Air Force information is accurate, we're way off in our provisions estimations. We're going to have to get back to Whelan to redo his weight calculations."

It wasn't really a question, so Atticus remained mute.

He was busy rechecking their ammunition requirements. As always, he erred on the side of being overprovisioned rather than under.

Older Atticus turned to Maggie. "Would the lady like to accompany me down to the dungeons to chat to Whelan and his fellow trolls?"

Not glancing up from her mission brief notes, Maggie replied, "I'm fine, thank you."

Atticus knew himself well enough to recognise the disappointment in his own countenance. While Older Atticus attempted to maintain his cheery disposition, there was clear despondency at Maggie's rejection. It wasn't her first rebuff.

"Right." Older Atticus straightened his back. "I'll go see what they have to say." He checked his watch. "The mess should be open. I'll pick us up something for lunch."

Atticus was about to tell his other self what he would like, but decided it was a pointless endeavour. Without another word, Older Atticus left. A hush descended on the room for a time.

Rubbing her neck, Maggie rolled her head around. "Tell me about the future. Anything. I think I need a distraction."

"Like what?"

"Anything. Maybe not *Star Trek* this time."

Atticus thought for a moment. "The thing you never expect about the future is how many passwords you're meant to remember. It's so fucking frustrating. And just when you can remember one off the top of your head they ask you to change it again. Or worse, *they* forget it and the password you've been using quite happily doesn't work anymore and you have to change it for no reason." He waggled a finger for effect. "Oh, but don't you dare try and change it to what you knew it was but they said it wasn't.

25

Why? Because it's already been used, apparently. Aha, you say, if that's the case then why doesn't it bloody work? That's the thing, automated systems of the future are never going to answer that question because they don't care." Atticus took a breath.

Maggie stared at him, mouth open. "It's really difficult sometimes to work out if you're making things up just to confuse me."

"Believe me, the future is confusing enough without me adding to it."

She absentmindedly picked at her tights; it was clear something else was on her mind. After a minute of silence, she spoke. "He needs to get his own place."

Atticus turned to Maggie. She was looking at her briefing papers, face neutral.

"He? As in..." He jerked his head towards the door through which the other Atticus had exited. "Is he annoying you?"

"No." Her face crinkled in the adorable way it did whenever she didn't want to talk about what she was about to talk about. "Just the opposite." She moaned. "When he's close, out of pure instinct I reach for his hand, *your* hand. I know I shouldn't, but he's you. But he's not you. But he is, kind of. It's, uh... confusing. Frustrating." She threw her hands up. "Everything!"

Maggie's dilemmas echoed his own. The man was so familiar, so known, yet logic dictated he was an outsider. None of this felt right.

"I can also see it from his side, I mean, my side." Atticus laughed at the absurdity of his own words. "If one day I turned around and we were no longer together *and* you were there right in front of me, I'd be devastated. I don't care how many logic knots I tied myself into, it would rip me apart."

"So, what?" Maggie crinkled her forehead. "You share me, is that it?"

"Oh god, no. That's insane for all concerned."

"Then what?" There wasn't anger or malice in her question, just genuine enquiry. She was just as out to sea as he was. "Are there always going to be two of you? Two Atticuses?"

Atticus shrugged. "Look at it this way," he did his best to plaster on a smile, "at least you'll always have a spare."

"That's not funny."

Atticus saw the pain in her eyes. His flippancy wasn't helping. "Sorry. This is really weird for all of us." He inhaled deeply. "I assume he's stuck here. If we manage to pull this off," he motioned to the set of plans before them, "then he'll have no timeline to return to. Sending him forward would only create the same problem we have now: two of me. It's..." Atticus rubbed his temple. "It's fucked up is what it is."

Maggie nodded, not disagreeing. Their talk hadn't resolved anything, but it had at least brought their troubling thoughts out in the open. No matter what, the two of them were a team. They communicated well, sharing the good, the bad and the confusing. It's what kept them close.

Again, Younger Atticus was reminded of what his older self had had taken away from him. Of the Maggie he couldn't have. Not for the first time, he wondered what had happened to the other Maggie, the one from Older Atticus's time. His other self still refused to say. Younger Atticus found it difficult to believe his counterpart could have just left her behind.

Beyond the intimacy confusion, there was another

aspect that Atticus found confounding. The other Atticus was him, yet there was certainly an element of suspicion in the older man's motives. Atticus knew his other self was hiding far more than he was letting on.

The old saying about knowing someone better than they knew themselves was twisted beyond all recognition for Atticus and his doppelganger. If Rathdowne were to give their plan the go ahead, the two of them would be leaping into a most dangerous mission. Younger Atticus realised he didn't have all the intelligence he'd want, because his other self was holding back.

He wondered just how much his other self wasn't telling him.

"I don't like it in the slightest."

Rathdowne sat behind his desk in his new office inside the Tower of London. His moustache positively bristled. To avoid extra aggravation, Older Atticus was holed up in their office awaiting the outcome.

For the last hour Younger Atticus and Maggie had presented their plan. The room was strewn with charts, diagrams, timelines and lists. They'd had a revolving door of experts, including SAS officers, two meteorologists, an aviation consultant and a US Air Force Colonel.

In the moments following that first statement after hearing their proposal, Rathdowne stewed in aggravated silence, but it wasn't hard to tell what he was thinking. The man's default setting was irritable. Especially when it came to Atticus. Two Atticuses, doubly so.

It had taken them the better part four days to work out the finer details before they'd been ready to present the plan to Rathdowne. Now that they'd done so, given the man's silent response, it seemed likely their efforts had been in vain.

"This has to be the most insane operation I've ever seen." Rathdowne shifted in his seat. "And that's really saying something. I've seen all your other operations, Wolfe." He motioned for the two of them to sit. "I... I wasn't expecting that. I would have thought the first priority would have been nabbing Preston before he installs his own man into the Kremlin. If everything occurs like your other self said, then surely Preston should be the main target. Then we worry about your time-travelling mate."

"Without my time-travelling *mate*," the word stuck in Atticus's throat, "we risk even greater failure."

"Greater than the ashes of Saigon?"

There was no waver or hitch in Atticus's response. "Yes."

Rathdowne frowned and folded his arms. "Explain."

"Imagine this." Maggie leaned forward, taking up the thread. "We go and put a halt to Oliver's evil plans. Yay us. We have a victory party and while we're all nursing hangovers and wondering where our pants are, Oliver jumps in his little time machine and stops our plan before it even begins."

"Oh shit."

"Quite an astute observation." Atticus tilted his head approvingly. "We have two fronts in this war. The one where Oliver is messing with events he doesn't understand, and the other, where he succeeds in creating a functioning time machine, which ironically also causes him to mess with events he doesn't understand. Either one will have devastating consequences beyond measure for the world. Option one, well, we've heard what happens: the start of a nuclear war that's not going to be good for anyone, except maybe the cockroaches. The second could be even worse. The world could become Oliver's plaything. He'd have the ability to go backwards and forwards in time, endlessly attempting to manipulate events. Billions could die. It was bad enough when he was trying to manipulate one time-line. Imagine if he had access to them all."

Atticus hadn't thought it was possible for Rathdowne to become any whiter. He was wrong. Atticus spoke as calmly as he could manage. "Sir Francis Bacon hit the nail on the head when he said knowledge itself is power. It's at the very core of the spy business." Atticus straightened his back. "And that means that right now, Oliver is the most powerful man alive. We can't let him win. The world literally depends on us succeeding."

Rathdowne growled. "Life was far simpler before you arrived, Wolfe."

"I'm not disagreeing with you."

"That's a change."

It was plain Rathdowne was weighing up the outcomes of the various choices before him. Do nothing and he'd be responsible for either nuclear Armageddon or the erasure of history. Proceed with the plan and the first two could still potentially occur, as well as an out-and-out war with the Soviet Union should it go balls up.

Atticus didn't envy Rathdowne at that moment. There was no one for him to defer to. No one higher up the chain of command who could understand where the intelligence had come from. There was no way to tell his superiors his dilemma without sounding like a madman. This was on Rathdowne's shoulders alone. It wasn't often a middle management bureaucrat was literally responsible the fate of the world.

The pale man lifted his heavy head. "Fine. You have a go mission." He hoisted a palm to silence their thanks before they voiced them. "But you listen here, Wolfe. If you start World War Three, leave my name out of it."

"I'll do my best." Wolfe raised an eyebrow. "But I can't promise anything."

THREE

"What's a five-letter word for dull?"

"Basingstoke."

Older Atticus put down the newspaper and stared at himself incredulously. "Doesn't fit."

The younger Atticus shrugged. "True, though."

The two were on a commercial BOAC flight to East Germany, set to meet the remainder of their team. Older Atticus had been working on the crossword since take-off, half an hour before.

"Remember the Marsden do?"

"Ugh." Older Atticus grunted without taking his eyes off the newspaper. "There's fifty hours of one night in Basingstoke we'll never get back."

Atticus still found it difficult to believe he was talking to himself. He wasn't the only one. The side glances he'd received from their fellow passengers told him they'd been noticed. They were not only identical, but possessed the exact same mannerisms. Little did their fellow passengers realise there was a good reason for that, but the explanation would require significantly more alcohol than the Vickers VC10 could safely carry.

In an attempt to counter confusion, Older Atticus had started to grow a beard. It wasn't fully formed, but it was on its way. Younger Atticus had lobbied for a goatee, but his older self refused to go the full evil-Spock look.

Younger Atticus found it amusing that even though the two were spies on a clandestine mission, MI6 still insisted they fly BOAC, the precursor to British Airways. He'd argued that British spies flying a British airline would be conspicuous. The counter argument was that they were supporting their economy and it would save the taxpayer money. Atticus thought the fact they were flying first class somewhat diluted the argument.

Flying in the sixties was a different experience to the mass-market, cattle-transport of the twenty-first century; it had a sense of glamour. Leaving the country was a luxury few could afford, especially on a plane. Every step of the process screamed indulgence, as if every passenger was experiencing something unique, exclusive. They even had lemon-scented towels.

The hostesses—for they were universally female—were all young and attractive. The captain greeted the first-class passengers personally before take-off. Disconcertingly for Atticus, he'd kept the cockpit door open during the flight. Passengers could pop in for a visit if they were so inclined, and everyone could see the instruments, and the flight crew casually going about their business. The whole scene was an anathema for someone from the post-9/11 world.

As much as he tried, Younger Atticus just couldn't feel comfortable in his other self's company. He was sure there would be a planet full of psychologists who'd love to dissect that one.

He put a lot of it down to the fact that his older self had so far divulged little about what had happened to him in the preceding year. Apart from the bare minimum tales of mass destruction, he'd remained tight lipped. As far as Young Atticus was concerned, his reticence went beyond the purported intention of not wanting to mess with the timeline and bordered on evasion to the point of deception.

There was more to the story than Older Atticus was letting on, and Younger Atticus didn't like not knowing all the relevant information. The fact that he was keeping it from himself was the most infuriating aspect. *How could you not trust yourself?*

There was something going on, but his constant probing of his slightly older self had revealed nothing. Older Atticus was familiar with his own interrogation techniques, and knew how to counter them.

Regardless, Younger Atticus would keep probing. He needed answers, any answers. Sitting and stewing on this lack of information while his other self nonchalantly read the paper wasn't going to get him those answers. He may as well start somewhere.

"Is it possible someone else could come back in time? From where you came from?"

"No."

"You seem pretty certain of that."

"I am."

This last response was given so emphatically it was clear that line of questioning was dead. That in itself was interesting. Did he leave instructions for the machine to be destroyed after he left? If so, how could Older Atticus be certain his orders were carried out? The more time Younger Atticus spent in his other self's company, the less he knew. That didn't mean he wouldn't keep trying.

"Are you intending on going home?"

Older Atticus turned to him. "I went home but someone was already there."

"Your own home."

Older Atticus narrowed his eyes. "It *is* my home."

Trying to keep his annoyance from his tone and surely failing, Younger Atticus said, "To your own home in your *own* time."

"Too many nuclear explosions for my liking." Older Atticus leaned back in his chair. "Tends to keep one up at night."

"So, you're staying?"

"I don't have much of a choice." He lowered his voice. "No time machine."

Younger Atticus didn't care for his own condescending tone.

His older self went on. "Plus, I have a world to save. *We* have a world to save." He groaned. "And I have to finish this crossword. What's a five-letter word for an act of remaining in the air in one place?"

It was this kind of evasiveness that infuriated Atticus. Every time he asked a straightforward question it was deflected, sidestepped or point-blank rejected. It was beyond annoying.

Younger Atticus ground his teeth. "Twat."

"No, needs to start with an h. And that's only four letters."

"You're a twat."

"I'm you."

"Then I'm a twat."

Older Atticus held up his palms. "If you say so."

"I do. You do. We do." Younger Atticus rubbed his eyes. "This is ridiculous."

Folding the newspaper into his lap, Older Atticus sighed. "You're the one who wanted to spell twat with an h."

"Doesn't it bother you?"

"Yes. It really does. It needs to end in an r."

"You're maddening." He held up a hand. "We're maddening." Taking a moment to steady himself, Younger Atticus went on as calmly as he could. "You're giving me nothing. What makes it worse is you know exactly how fucking annoying it is. You completely know it, yet you're still giving me absolutely nothing. Do you not trust me? Because if that's the case that's fucking nuts. *We're* nuts."

"It's not that."

"Then what is it? I genuinely want to know."

Older Atticus sighed again, but this time it was softer, not a sigh of annoyance. "Ever since I got to the sixties, *we* got to the sixties, we've screwed everything up. Oliver never would have been discovered. Latvia never would have happened. Oliver's ascension in the Soviet ranks. MI6 being blown up, Saigon and the rest of it, none of that would have happened if Muggins here," he pointed to the both of them, "hadn't plopped down in the middle of Knightsbridge and started fucking about. That's a lot of destruction and chaos for one person. We can't add to that. If it offends you, I'm sorry, but I'm keeping it to myself so I don't somehow make it worse."

"Is that possible?"

"What if we somehow keep flared trousers from going out of style? What if *Ghostbusters* never gets made? What if we cause Limp Bizkit to become the biggest band in the world?"

Both Atticuses shivered at the same time.

"Okay, fine." Younger Atticus folded his arms. "I guess

there are worse things than nuclear Armageddon." He paused, regarding his slightly older self. "*Saigon and the rest of it.* That's what you said, those were your exact words. Does that mean there are more cities that fall? It's not just Saigon?"

"Did you not hear the bit about Limp Bizkit?"

"There's that evasiveness again. But really, can you give me anything more?"

Older Atticus's facial features hardened once again. "No. Because of—"

"... the timeline. So you keep saying."

"I keep saying it but you don't seem to hear it."

"Oh, I hear it but it just sounds like bullshit."

"I'm not the one arguing with myself, mate."

"Yes, you are."

They fell into another awkward silence. Older Atticus resumed his crossword puzzle. Younger Atticus had other things on his mind.

IN A DARK AND disused part of Rhein-Main Air Base outside of Frankfurt, three men waited in the cold. The USAF air base was the primary airfield used during the Berlin airlift. Tonight, it had a very different function.

It had just gone nine and Younger Atticus, Doyle and Cohen stood on a windswept field awaiting lift-off. Despite their high-altitude suits they shivered with cold and were well on their way to miserable.

"Just once I'd like a mission to Acapulco. Or Hawaii." Cohen wrapped his arms around himself. "Hell, I'd settle for Blackpool at this stage."

The boisterous Cohen and lanky Doyle were highly

experienced and decorated MI6 veterans and, as Atticus had experienced firsthand, damn handy in a scrap. In their last mission behind the Iron Curtain the two had been invaluable. For Atticus, having them as part of this operation was a no brainer and he was glad to have them. Although, going by the freezing trepidation on their faces, he wasn't sure the feeling was mutual.

The two had arrived twenty minutes earlier. Cohen had been extracted from a mission in Ghana where he'd been assessing the Soviet influence in the newly independent Commonwealth country. Doyle came in from Finland, where he'd been recruiting members of the local Communist Party. After exchanging warm greetings, Atticus had given them a rundown of the mission. Their initial response had been stunned silence. They followed that up with gobsmacked before moving on to bewildered.

Cohen poured whiskey into small coloured anodised cups while the three danced from one foot to the other, trying to keep their circulation going. They patiently awaited the commander for their unconventional flight. Atticus hadn't met the man. By all accounts he was eccentric, but good at his job. In fact, he was the only one who could perform the job.

It was the other passenger Atticus was most concerned about; specifically, what Cohen and Doyle's reactions would be.

The three engaged in banter while trying to keep warm. Atticus saw the two figures crossing the airfield first. The one in uniform was average height and strode with arrogance. The second was the Older Atticus.

As the two walked towards the craft, Doyle and Cohen openly stared. Whiplash looks darted from Older to Younger Atticus and back again.

Doyle put down his cup. "Cohen, my lad, what the hell was in that whiskey?"

As if jolted by electricity, Cohen stood up. "There's bleedin' two of you?"

Older Atticus waved to the men warmly then halted, remembering his role. He feigned a genial nice-to-meet-you tone. "I'm Atticus's brother, Robert. Now, which one of you is Cohen and which one's Doyle?"

Dumbfounded, the two men managed to string enough words together to introduce themselves. Older Atticus leaned forward, pretending he was hearing the information for the first time. Younger Atticus thought he was over-doing the performance. It was hard to tell from their shocked expressions exactly what the other agents thought.

With a wave of his palm, Older Atticus said, "May I introduce Captain Bukowski of the US Airforce."

"That's Screaming Jack Bukowski, boys." The man's Southern accent was as thick as molasses. "But you can call me Screaming Jack. A pleasure." He vigorously shook their hands. "I have to say, y'all are the most stupid crazy ass sons of bitches who ever graced God's green earth."

"Thanks?" Doyle appeared to still be in shock.

The man they were meant to call Screaming Jack led them inside the craft, through a small pressurised door with its spinning wheel lock. Normally, a bright orange vessel would not be chosen for a spy mission, but they had little choice in the matter. The capsule was more like a submarine than an aircraft. That was because it served a similar function to a submarine; it was designed to keep the occupants from getting the bends and/or exploding from the inside out.

The pressurised gondola sat beside three balloons that were in the process of being inflated. The vessel, which would take them far above the Soviet Union, was little more than a pressurised tube, barely big enough for the five of them and mission supplies. Outside, gas tanks were strapped to the outer hull for the balloon's long flight. There were tiny round portals that served as windows, but other than that, it was just one giant orange metal tube.

Screaming Jack had been selected because he was the only member of NATO who had flown anything remotely like this. After ushering them into the tiny confines of the craft he proceeded to check dials and instruments. But Cohen and Doyle's attention was focused elsewhere.

Cohen folded his arms. "You never mentioned a brother."

"I never mentioned I can swing dance either." It was true, he'd taken it up for a brief period in the early 2000s. It didn't last long. "Rob's been in the SAS for years, thought it was time he went on a real mission."

Older Atticus took up the thread. "I thought skydiving behind the Iron Curtain and fighting half the Red Army would be a nice holiday from actually dangerous missions. It was either that or a weekender in the Lakes District."

The brotherly banter seemed to go some way towards convincing Cohen and Doyle. It wasn't like they had an alternative take. They were unlikely to suspect that this new Atticus was a version of Atticus from a year ahead, sent back to prevent nuclear annihilation indirectly caused by Atticus's accidental arrival from his own time in the twenty-first century. Really, who would believe that?

The Captain finished his checks and turned to the group, letting out a low whistle. "Now that Robert here has told me your real mission, I have to say I think y'all are nuttier than a squirrel turd, but if anyone can pull this off it's Screaming Jack Bukowski." He clapped his hands. "Let's get goin'. I've got the first hundred thousand feet to give you boys a crash course in high-altitude skydiving."

Cohen raised a finger. "Please don't say crash."

Ignoring Cohen, Screaming Jack went on. "Any you boys skydived before?"

All four put up their hands.

"Good, good. What flight experience y'all got?"

"I've had a few flying lessons," Younger Atticus said with a shrug, "but only a few. I managed to learn how to take off and fly around for a bit, but we never got to the landing part."

Younger Atticus—and, by definition, his older counterpart—had taken flying lessons years ago in an enthusiastic attempt at a new hobby. It hadn't stuck, and they only logged a few dozen flying hours before moving on to the next thing. Possibly swing dancing. Atticus probably couldn't tell the difference between an altitude indicator and a direction finder now.

Screaming Jack sneered. "Some might call the landing the most important part, son."

"Lucky we're not flying a plane then, isn't it?"

Screaming Jack was beginning to rub Atticus the wrong way.

The Captain slapped his hands together. "Well, now. Let's get these balloons fully stuffed like my mamma's Thanksgiving turkey and get us into the wild black yonder."

It was another half hour before the three massive silver balloons were fully inflated. Captain Jack spun the wheel to seal them into the pressurised craft. Atticus couldn't help but feel like he was being sealed into a coffin.

They would fly high into East German airspace, then over Czechoslovakia, Eastern Europe and high above the heart of the USSR—high enough to avoid Soviet radar detection. They would be at a higher altitude than a U2. The plane, not the band.

Their target was deep inside Siberia, home to harsh, unforgiving terrain with even harsher and less forgiving adversaries between them and their target: Ganim.

When planning had begun for this mission there had been all sorts of wild suggestions thrown about, including everything from launching their mission from a submarine into the Black Sea to flying a B52 into the middle of Siberia. The plane, not the band.

One idea that briefly gained traction was to try their luck taking the Trans-Siberian Railway and leaping from the train at some point. But as foreigners, they would have been watched the entire way, and four missing passengers would have been detected soon enough. The Soviets would have scoured the countryside, putting the whole region on alert. It was too much of a risk. And as the balloon-powered pressurised metal vessel lifted into the pitch-black night, Atticus laughed at the thought that this was the safer option.

For days they'd argued for Maggie to come on the mission, but the US Airforce had vehemently rallied against the idea. Every logical point Atticus made was shot down. In the end it was moot anyway; they don't make flight suits for women. Feeling colder by the second, knowing full well the immense danger that faced them and observing Screaming Jack Bukowski's manic eagerness, for once Atticus was glad Maggie wasn't accompanying them.

For all his bravado and Southern homilies, Screaming Jack knew his shit. As the balloon made its rapid ascent, he adjusted their altitude suits and provided them with expert knowledge about the nuances of high-altitude ascents. He was a natural instructor, knowledgeable and patient, and his expertise put them a little more at ease.

The Atticuses had their skydiving C licence with over two hundred jumps between them. Cohen and Doyle were both well experienced, and had parachuted behind enemy lines on several occasions. However, none of them had dived from the height they'd be attempting on this mission, primarily because only one man had ever been mad enough to try.

Five years before, Air Force Captain Joe Kittinger parachuted from an altitude of 102,800 feet, more than 19 miles. Screaming Jack had sought approval for the record-breaking jump, as well as designing the rig. He was also Kittinger's commanding officer. Atticus was sure Kittinger's record had held for at least another fifty years. But their jumps today would be higher—quite literally from the stratosphere.

If they picked up the jet streams, Screaming Jack estimated that the journey would take them seven hours. They'd reach terra firma just before dawn. Apparently if they landed within ten miles of their target, the jump would be considered a success. As far as Atticus was concerned, if they survived the flight at all it would be a minor miracle.

Screaming Jack would fly on after the others had jumped, maintaining the high altitude until he was out of Soviet airspace. If for some reason he was forced to crash land, he could claim a system failure. With Atticus and his team gone there would be no espionage or surveillance equipment aboard. He could claim he had simply wandered off course. Quite a long way off course. They all hoped it didn't come to that and that he'd make his rendezvous in the Philippines Sea.

In the small confines of the white-walled gondola, Screaming Jack went through his instructions for the high-altitude jump several times, carefully discussing the nuances, parachute design and how to deploy the secondary chute. "Now, y'all have used chutes before and that's fine. But that's not yer biggest worry. Hypoxia is. That's why I'm introducing more oxygen into the cabin. We'll be at 100 per cent oxygen by the time we reach twenty thousand feet. I have to flush the nitrogen from yer blood-stream or y'all will get caisson disease." He saw their blank faces and added, "The bends, boys. Believe me, that's some-thin' ya want to avoid. If any o' you suffer from decompression sickness you could die or wind up permanently disabled from nitrogen bubbles in yer bloodstream. And I haven't even mentioned frostbite—you'll be hitting negative ninety-five Fahrenheit in freefall. But then again, if you're unconscious when you hit the ground because you were unable to open yer chute, frostbite ain't gonna be botherin' you much, now is it?"

After that pep talk Screaming Jack went back to his instruments and the men fell into a contemplative silence. Searching for a topic of discussion other than certain death, Younger Atticus motioned to Cohen and Doyle.

"Thanks for volunteering for the mission, guys."

Cohen gave him a friendly salute. "I'd follow you anywhere, Atticus Wolfe."

Younger Atticus gave a dip of his head in thanks. "That's loyalty."

"No," Cohen's face danced with mischief, "more morbid curiosity."

"Funny."

Doyle poked his lanky elbow towards Older Atticus.

"What's your story, Robert? What brings you here with your crazy-arse brother?"

"I was going to crack a joke, but I might go with morbid curiosity too."

The other two laughed. Atticus couldn't put his finger on why, but something about the Older Atticus getting a laugh out of his fellow agents made him uncomfortable. In fact, even having him on the mission made him uncomfortable. For some reason he just couldn't bring himself to trust the other Atticus. Deep down he understood that was ludicrous. After all, it was him, not some alternate-universe goatee-wearing evil doppelganger—it was actually *him*. Yet, despite all logic, Atticus felt uneasy in his other self's presence.

What was likely making the whole situation worse was Maggie. Older Atticus was obviously infatuated with her. There was no denying the man's lingering gazes, the puppy dog eyes he gave her when he thought no one was looking. But there was also a strong sense of melancholy.

Atticus couldn't miss the prolonged glances the other man had given his girlfriend. If it were anyone else he would have called him out, told him to stop lusting after the woman he loved. But again, it wasn't that simple. They were the same looks *he* gave Maggie. He could understand the other man because he *was* the other man. If someone suddenly told Younger Atticus he couldn't love Maggie, touch her, need her, there was no way he could just stop, especially when she was right there in front of him.

To his credit, Older Atticus had done his best to keep his distance, to avoid complicating matters any more than they already were. He never attempted to become too close with Maggie, though it was plain that he dearly wanted to. He spent his nights on the couch. More than once, Atticus had caught him glancing longingly at Maggie as she slept.

It was infuriating that Younger Atticus could be both aggravated and sympathetic at the same time. If he could just settle on one emotion, be it anger, distrust or acceptance, it would be a lot easier. But life wasn't that simple. *His* life certainly wasn't.

As Atticus watched his other self casually chatting with Cohen, he couldn't help but feel he trusted Older Atticus less than he did the other agents on the mission. It was illogical, but there it was. Their chat on the plane had done little to dissuade the unease coursing through him.

A lot could happen to a man in a year, and it was plain Older Atticus had been through a hell of a lot. The problem was, Atticus had no idea what any of those experiences were.

As Atticus watched Screaming Jack tinker with the dials and the other men settle in to rest before the mission, he couldn't deny his feeling of unease. The team he'd selected should have filled him with confidence that the mission would be a success. But instead, he felt mounting dread.

CHAPTER
FOUR

Younger Atticus watched the altimeter pass sixty-five thousand feet. He felt slightly lightheaded and oddly euphoric—probably due to the increased levels of oxygen. They'd strategically gone south of East Germany to gain more altitude before crossing over.

Screaming Jack let them know they were now flying high above Czechoslovakia.

Collectively, the grown men all giggled at the flying high comment. Atticus didn't feel any great trepidation at having passed into Soviet airspace. Perhaps it was the increased oxygen that helped.

Now behind the Iron Curtain—or rather, above it—Atticus's thoughts turned to Ganim. Once, he'd chased the man across the globe, and now he was doing it again, albeit in a different century.

Since arriving in this period he'd only spoken to Ganim on a few occasions, all of them tense. For Atticus it had only been a short amount of time since he'd been tasked with chasing down the terrorist, an assignment that became an obsession. For Ganim, half a century had passed. Atticus rubbed his temple.

According to the intelligence they had, Ganim was holed up in a facility deep inside Siberia. Oliver wanted his asset well protected and far away from spy-riddled Moscow. What he had Ganim working on was unknown, but their sources in Siberia reported that many trucks with electronics had travelled into the compound and returned empty. The only logical conclusion was that Oliver had him creating his own time machine. Whether Ganim's involvement was voluntary remained to be seen.

Armed with a history book describing the latter half of the twentieth century, with a man who'd not only lived through that period but also knew how to manipulate all of time, Oliver was incredibly dangerous. He stood by what he'd told Rathdowne: Oliver Preston was the most dangerous man on the planet. Possibly ever.

The key to stopping him was getting to Ganim. Whether he lived or died would be up to Ganim himself. If somehow he'd become a convert to Oliver's cause, Atticus would have no choice but to kill him. He'd be too dangerous to be allowed to live. If he was there against his will, Atticus would have to decide if he would come back with them or not. As much as Atticus wanted to return to his own time, if he had to decide between his own selfish desire and the fate of the world, well, there wasn't much choice. The world came first.

It seemed Atticus wasn't the only one wrestling with his thoughts. The others seemed restless, on edge. Screaming Jack checked the instruments and made a few adjustments. They had hours before they would be over the target, but it seemed their minds were already deep inside Siberian territory.

Younger Atticus cracked his knuckles. "I suppose we should talk mission specifics, then?" Cohen and Doyle sat up. They'd only received rudimentary briefings so far. "Our target is a yet to be completed nuclear reactor in central Siberia." He lamented not being able to sweep clutter off a table and lay out blueprints. Their cramped confines negated such dramatic activities. Instead, he handed around black and white photographs that had been taken by the CIA a month ago on a routine surveillance run. "As you can see, the walls and roof are up, but no reactor is in place. All nuclear engineers have been sent home until further notice. Nuclear power is no longer the site's function. Unfortunately for us, security weren't given the same orders. Four guard towers and, if they stick to the same routine as when the CIA was there, twelve-hour shifts. That's good for us because I don't care how good a guard you are, after twelve hours your attention is shot. As far as we can tell, they're guarding just one man: Omar Ganim." Younger Atticus handed them a photofit he'd put together of Ganim. It wasn't a bad likeness. "He's an inventor who has his own laboratory and resources within the facility. He's our primary target. We take him alive at all costs. If that's not an option, we don't leave unless he's confirmed dead. Is that understood?" Atticus waited for nods from them all, his other self included. "Secondary is to destroy any and all equipment and research at the facility."

Doyle inhaled and then asked, "What's he building in there?"

It was the one question Atticus had been hoping they wouldn't ask.

"I'm afraid to say at this stage it's a need-to-know situation."

Shaking his head, Cohen scoffed. "Of course it is. Why would we need to know? We're just the muscle."

Atticus turned to Doyle. "I assume you have enough explosives for the job?"

Doyle chuckled. "I've enough to blast a hole in the moon."

Screaming Jack spun around in alarm. "You brought volatile materials on my rig?"

Batting his eyelids, Doyle responded, "I was going to invade a hostile country's fiercely defended secret fortress with a packet of crisps, but in the end I thought explosives seemed the more sensible option."

"You realise this is a pressurised environment? We're stuck in here with your toys with no escape. You do know chemical compounds change with pressure and altitude?"

Doyle gave him a flippant wave of his hand. "By the time we realise there's cause to be concerned we'll all be holding harps and sporting wings."

With a newly minted sense of alarm slapped across his features, Screaming Jack shook his head slowly. "I'm glad I'm not going on this damn fool thing with you lot. Sounds like a suicide mission if y'all ask me."

Older Atticus frowned. "You should do motivational talks. You're an inspirational leader." He splayed his hand across his chest. "I for one feel emboldened by your heart-felt encouraging words."

Completely missing the sarcasm, Screaming Jack winked as if to say, *you're welcome*. Glancing between the two Atticuses, he shook his head and chuckled. "They'll never expect there'd be two o' yers. Heh. Gonna mess with those Commies, I plum reckon. They won't know whether to check their asses or scratch their watches. Good for you boys."

At the same time, both Atticuses replied, "Don't call me boy."

Cohen and Doyle sat up, knowing Atticus well enough to know when he was riled. In this case, riled times two.

Screaming Jack threw up a placating palm. "Aw, now, I got no problem with niggers, fought beside 'em in World War Two. Hell of a bunch of fighters. Hellcats, they were. You're alright by me. Just keep away from my sister."

He laughed uproariously and slapped Doyle on the arm. Cohen's eyes went wide in alarm. No one else laughed. Doyle stood as best he could in the confoned space, positioning himself between Screaming Jack and the fuming Atticuses.

The man was their only means of making their drop zone. Hell, he was the only one currently keeping them alive. That didn't mean Atticus wasn't fantasising about pushing him out the pressurised gondola, wondering if he'd see the error of his ways on the twelve-mile plummet to his inevitable and gruesome death.

Older Atticus straightened his back. "Mr Bukowski…"

"Screaming Jack, please, Rob." He was recovering from his bout of self-imposed laughter.

Clenching his jaw, Older Atticus went on. "Mr Bukowski, I know you think you're being complimentary but you need to know that the use of the n word, coupled with… everything you've just said, is highly offensive. I absolutely recommend you don't repeat it, or anything of the sort. In fact—"

"Oh come on, I was just joshin'. Ain't no harm in anything. It's a joke."

Older Atticus raised himself up. "No, it's not a joke. It's an exercise in privilege and in ensuring the likes of us," he motioned to Atticus and himself, "are continually reminded of our position. Which, let's be honest here, is generally at the heel of a boot. So, I recommend you take your jokes, as you put it, and either stick them up your arse or I'll forcibly shove them down your fucking throat. Do I make myself clear?"

"I was only—"

"Do. I. Make. Myself. Clear?"

Atticus had never seen himself get angry. That wasn't to say he never got angry—thanks to the colour of his skin and the life he'd led, he'd fought much of his life. But it was a completely different experience to see it happen from the outside. Even though it was another version of himself espousing fury, Atticus had to admit he felt slightly intimidated. A completely odd sensation.

For all of Screaming Jack's bluster and vitriol he seemed to realise he'd gone too far and, more importantly, that he was in danger. He held aloft both palms, uttered a mumbling apology and went back to fiddling with the dials, no doubt hoping that would be the end of it.

As much as Younger Atticus wanted to push him to his death, Screaming Jack was the only one who understood how the gear worked and could get them safely to the drop zone. Pain him as it might, they needed the racist Yank. His counterpart's silent anger indicated that Older Atticus was traversing similar thoughts.

They all fell into an awkward silence.

Partly to avoid further discussion, Younger Atticus suggested they all get some sack time. They'd need the rest for the mission to come.

Two hours later, Atticus was woken by a kick to his foot. He'd been dreaming of an old mission to Istanbul with a madman called Charles Bishop. The details of the dream wilted away as soon as he saw Doyle's face.

"We've got a problem."

Younger Atticus soon found the source of the problem: Screaming Jack Bukowski.

"When did it start?"

Cohen shook the man's shoulders. His eyes were glazed and unfocused.

"About half an hour ago. He couldn't seem to finish his sentences, and then after about fifteen minutes he just babbled gibberish. Then... this."

The comatose man was white, stiff as a board and foam leaked from the corner of his mouth. His breathing was shallow.

It was hypobaric hypoxia. It didn't matter if it was his first ascent or his hundredth. Gaining altitude too rapidly didn't allow the body enough time to adjust to the reduced oxygen and changes in air pressure. Screaming Jack seemed to have succumbed to the very thing he had warned them about.

Older Atticus shone a torch into Screaming Jack's eyes but got no reaction. "I'm guessing nitrogen bubbles got in his bloodstream and made their way to his brain. Unless anyone has a hyperbaric chamber in their back pocket there's not much we can do but..."

In his hand he held a morphine syringe. There wasn't much of an alternative. Even if they abandoned their mission and somehow could fly the balloon to a friendly country, that could take days. Screaming Jack didn't have days. He had minutes.

The Younger Atticus's face contorted into grim determination and he nodded to his other self. They couldn't save the man on the brink of death. No chance of medical help. No way to save him. There was only one thing for it. Leaving that gruesome task to Older Atticus, he turned his attention to Doyle, hunched over the wall of dials and gauges.

"We're on the right bearing, right altitude. As far as I can make out we're on course." Doyle rubbed his stubbled chin. "I think." He gave Younger Atticus a faint smile. "I'm not an expert on any of this. It looks like we've well and truly passed Moscow, passed Kazan. If I'm reading this right, we should be getting ready for the jump."

Atticus considered the now motionless Screaming Jack. "How exactly do we do that?"

All four men exchanged expectant glances. No one had an answer.

TWENTY MINUTES later all four stood in their white high-altitude jump suits, full astronaut-like helmets with oxygen tanks attached. They really did appear like they were on their way to space, which, in fact, they were. They'd checked one another's gear, connections and seals. Once they'd exchanged thumbs ups, they looked at one another nervously.

Their craft would continue on its way, Screaming Jack Bukowski included, and would likely crash somewhere in the Pacific Ocean. There was no spy equipment aboard. If it didn't make the ocean and the Soviets somehow found it, the US would claim it was a prototype that had floated off course.

Their target was just north of a small town called Tyukalinsk, deep inside Siberia, a hundred kilometres northwest of Omsk, the administrative centre of the region.

"We just set a record, boys." Doyle tapped one of the gauges. "One hundred and three thousand feet. We're just about to beat Air Force Captain Joe Kittinger's high altitude record. Nineteen miles straight down."

"It's not the jump I'm worried about," Cohen muttered. "It's the landing."

Without their expert, they were flying blind. They'd received only rudimentary training, and were taking a wild guess as to what their drop point should be.

"Does this go first or last?" Cohen kicked their supplies box, attached to a chute of its own.

It held whatever gear they couldn't jump with: spare rations, extra ammunition, grappling equipment, their tents and escape craft. They couldn't afford for it to end up somewhere near Japan.

"I'll jump with it." Doyle stared at the large silver metal box for a while. "I'll pull its cord right before I pull mine."

"Is that what we're meant to do?" Cohen's voice was full of doubt.

"No idea." Doyle sniffed. "We're winging this."

"Yes." Cohen eyed the dead body on the floor. "Now is exactly the time we should be improvising."

Older Atticus grunted. "We don't exactly have a choice."

There was no arguing the point, so they shuffled towards the circular door at the end of the tube. Atticus pulled the lever Screaming Jack had told him was the equalising valve, then waited thirty seconds before wrenching the wheel to the only door on the vessel.

The rush of wind was like a sledgehammer to the face. Outside was pure black. Endless, unending black. Atticus turned to Doyle, who gave him a nod. It wasn't a confident nod. To call it a semi-confident nod would be an overstatement. Atticus decided it was a barely-viable-temperate-weak-ass nod.

Shuffling his legs until they dangled over the edge,

Younger Atticus stared out into the vast expanse of nothing. The stars were the only way to tell which way was up. Cohen and Doyle were close behind, with Older Atticus standing behind them, wearing the oddest expression, one his younger self couldn't immediately categorise.

They synchronised their watches to the second, then awaited the countdown to the top of the minute. When the second hand hit sixty, Atticus turned to his fellow agents, gave them a thumbs up and leapt into the void.

The freefall was disorientating and terrifying. He tumbled like he was in a washing machine, losing all sense of space. Only with the aid of the luminous artificial horizon strapped to his forearm did he know which way was up. He spent a long time whirling out of control before he stabilised into an arched position.

Of all Atticus's previous jumps, most were low altitude, which made for quick, stealthy insertions. This, by contrast, felt like hours. The wind was screaming in his icy ears despite the helmet, and the thin, freezing air tore through the suit designed to keep it out.

Being unable to see the ground made it worse; he couldn't gauge his progress, which just added to the petrifying nature of the jump. Atticus was relying on his antiquated glow-in-the-dark altimeter to tell him when to pull the chute. He would have preferred a GPS and a full electronic display, but it would have to do.

During the long freefall, Atticus felt his consciousness fading. In the sheer blackness, the altitude and the bitter cold he could feel himself starting to black out, but fought against it. He'd hate to hit the ground unconscious at seven hundred miles an hour. It would really put a crimp in his day.

Travelling at faster than the speed of sound, freefall was

a fraction over four-and-a-half minutes. Settling into the moment, he searched in vain for his fellow agents. He couldn't spot a single one. It felt like he was alone in the universe, destined to fall forever.

But he wouldn't. At seventeen thousand feet he pulled his chute. It was a prototype ram air parachute the US Airforce was testing, and it deployed perfectly. It would take another eight minutes before he reached the ground. Atticus manoeuvred his trajectory towards the landing zone. Using a compass and very broad mental calculations, he did his best to aim for the rendezvous point. He really did miss GPS.

As he fell, he continued to search for Cohen, Doyle or his other self, but the sky was free of any chutes. Was he off course or were they? Did they leap out when he did? Did they all black out and fail to open their chutes? Dread crept in. As he slowly swung beneath the canopy he had a long time to think about worst-case scenarios.

Eventually he descended through the clouds and caught sight of land beneath. The eerie quarter-moon lit the inhospitable snow-covered Siberian landscape, stretching endlessly in all directions. There was a barren, lifeless beauty to it.

Two hundred feet up, Atticus readied himself for landing. Picking a flat piece of land, clear of forestation, rock or anything else that could do him harm, he executed a textbook parachute landing fall. The snow was cold but welcoming. His legs felt like jelly, but he managed to stand.

Quickly stowing his chute and helmet, he readied his gear and trudged through the knee-high snow to their designated rendezvous point. With his Sterling Mark 4 machine gun at the ready, he made his way through a forested area to where he hoped to find the others.

There was no one there.

In the freezing pre-dawn light, he waited. And waited. No one came. He tried the radio but received nothing but static. Half an hour later Atticus heard a twig snap. He was immediately on high alert. Slowly, he crept towards the source of the sound, weapon raised at the ready.

Rounding a rocky outcrop, he spied footprints in the snow. But that shouldn't have been where his attention was focused.

The barrel of the gun was freezing against his temple.

"You're lucky I didn't take you for a rabbit."

He looked up to see his other self with a joyous self-satisfied grin at the end of a gun barrel. He could really be a smug son-of-a-bitch.

Atticus pushed the weapon out of his face. "Where are the others?"

"Right here."

Turning, Atticus saw Doyle and Cohen, the latter being held up by the former. Cohen was white as a sheet.

"What happened?"

"Didn't stick the landing." Cohen sucked in air through clenched teeth. "The Polish judge only gave me a three point two. It's all politics, you know?"

Unimpressed by Cohen's flippancy, Doyle said, "His leg's broken. We've put it in a splint, dosed him up on painkillers, but his mobility is shot to hell."

They all understood what that meant. He was out of the game.

"I'll be fine." Cohen did his best to appear casual. It fell like sack of Russian potatoes. "I can still shoot."

Atticus had no doubt.

The others had landed successfully, as had the box of supplies and, critically, their escape equipment. After a brief rest, they made their way to their target, Cohen on Doyle's back. The sun was rising and they'd soon be exposed.

They pitched their compact tents, covering them in snow. Making their way up a ridge overlooking the valley, they peered through binoculars and set their eyes on their objective for the first time.

The nuclear power station was not yet complete. In fact, it appeared it never would be. With the hulking outer concrete edifice in place, construction had halted months before. A new, far more sinister endeavour now resided inside. There was a main entrance where the workers would have arrived when the station was operational, and another large fissure on one wall where trucks entered. This was the construction entrance, a gaping wound in the concrete edifice.

A barbed wire-topped mesh fence circled the immense concrete structure. It was tall, and potentially electrified. Four guard towers overlooked the scene. All in all, it wasn't exactly what one would label inviting. Given what it protected, Younger Atticus gauged the defences as lacklustre. Then again, with the compound being located in the middle of Siberia it was likely the Soviets deemed it more than adequate. Atticus was only too happy to exploit their complacency.

The woods surrounding the compound were thick with snow-covered trees. The forested area reached as far as the eye could see. There were no nearby towns, no signs of human existence anywhere except for the stark concrete monolith and the road leading to it.

There were little signs of life around the great half-constructed goliath, but the lack of snow on the road showed that it was well-traversed. The only humans who could be seen were the guards manning the towers on each of the four corners. They appeared alert and dedicated.

Atticus put down his binoculars. "Fun fact: it's the same design as Chernobyl."

Older Atticus grunted. "Oh, that's just fucking marvellous."

Doyle shook his head. "What's so special about Chernobyl?"

"Ask me in twenty years."

"What do we do now?" Cohen's voice was strained.

"Eat, then sleep though the day."

"And then?"

Atticus smiled. "Raise hell."

FIVE

I t was just after eleven pm when the first explosion detonated.

Doyle had promised "modest" blasts. This was anything but modest. In fact, it was downright ostentatious. Though it certainly did live up to the promise of raising hell.

The main gate erupted in an explosion of red and orange light. The deafening blast sent startled birds scurrying into the sky for miles around. Seconds later, the westernmost guard tower fell with an explosion at the base of one its struts, followed by the fall of the eastern one. A third blast plunged the entire complex into darkness while also cutting the facility's communications to the outside world.

Older Atticus, with the aid of a stationary Cohen, attacked the third guard tower while Doyle and Younger Atticus took on the final one. Within minutes all outer security had been neutralised.

That was the known element, but they still had no idea what lay in wait for them inside. They were about to find out.

While Cohen took up a sniper's position, both Atticus's and Doyle assembled before the now-ruined front entrance. Armed with multiple Browning Hi-Power pistols and a Sterling submachine gun each, they strode towards the smouldering main gate.

This was not a standard MI6 operation. MI6 was meant to operate in the shadows; it was all about stealth, concealment and subterfuge. It wasn't about explosions and frontal attacks. This was not the MI6 way.

But given what was at stake, the rule book had not only been thrown out the window, it had been doused in petrol and set on fire. When the literal fate of the world depended on their success, rules no longer had meaning.

Submachine guns tucked into their shoulders, the three advanced on the smoking wreckage that had once been a ten-foot-tall wooden gate. No guards rushed towards them, no angry shouts warned them away. The station was silent. That didn't mean they were safe. Quite the opposite, in fact.

"I'll take the main entrance, you two..."

"Rob, you take the truck bay, I'll..."

The Atticuses glared at one another as they issued simultaneous orders. Doyle's head swivelled between the two, bemused. Being a tactician, choosing a strategic path came naturally to the Atticuses. In the office, their combined minds and lack of hierarchy enabled their overlapping ideas to coalesce into creative tactics. In the field, however, a clear lack of leadership could be fatal.

"Gents, I'm not looking to get in the middle of a family dispute..." Doyle seemed oddly amused, a welcome respite from the carnage of the guard towers only minutes before.

Squaring his jaw, Older Atticus said, "Apologies. I'll take the truck bay... Atticus." He narrowed his eyes. "As you ordered."

Younger Atticus knew himself well enough to know the words burned his counterpart's insides. As many of his supervisors had learned the hard way, Atticus wasn't a follower. He preferred to be out front, driving the win. It wasn't arrogance—well, perhaps it was, a little—but Atticus was often the smartest person in the room. It made sense for him to take the helm. Forcing his other self to be subservient when he was, quite literally, just as qualified as the man he was taking orders from must have stung.

Not having time to coddle egos, Younger Atticus moved onto more pressing matters. Issuing a sharp hand gesture, he directed his older self to the truck entrance and Doyle to accompany him to the main entrance. With a renewed sense of purpose, guns up, they stalked across the compound.

Watching his other self enter the wide concrete breach, Younger Atticus could tell from his own body language he was still pissed at being told how to run a mission. The steam positively radiated off him.

Sartre got it wrong. Hell wasn't other people. It's being forced to work with yourself.

Atticus hit the radio. "How we looking, Cohen?"

A static-filled reply came back. "All clear. It's as quiet as Doyle's bedroom out there."

Without glancing back Doyle gave the snow-covered forest behind him the two fingered salute. They'd soon lose comms. Once inside the concrete wall, they'd go radio silent until they emerged, effectively cutting themselves off from any early warning should reinforcements arrive.

"Good luck, boys." Cohen's voice crackled. "See you on the other side."

Doyle and Atticus approached the main entrance. It was

on a small rise of steps. The huge double doors below the hammer and sickle gave the place a sense of Soviet majesty.

Doyle extracted a shotgun and blasted all four hinges. The doors fell with a matching sense of majesty.

Once the dust and echo of the gunshots died away, the inside of the building was dark and tomb-like. The two men swivelled their weapons, ready for any adversary, but there were none.

The front room was bare. What would become a reception area or a security checkpoint was currently just a large empty room. It was a good forty yards to the two sets of doors at the far end of the empty concrete chamber. That was a lot of ground to traverse without any cover whatsoever. They were exposed and vulnerable.

"I don't like this."

Atticus scanned the far doors over the barrel of his submachine gun. In a low voice he replied, "Me either. Feels like we're walking into a trap."

"You had to say it out loud, didn't you?"

As his steps echoed far too loudly in the cavernous expanse, Younger Atticus tilted his head towards Doyle without taking his eyes off the distant doors. "You wouldn't happen to have any Mabels on you, would you?"

Although he couldn't see it, Atticus could virtually hear Doyle's smile. "As a matter of fact, I do."

After rummaging around his webbing briefly, Doyle rolled a large home-made hockey puck-like device along the ground. It hit the far wall with a *clunk* and fell on its side. For a few seconds, nothing happened.

A burst of unmistakable AK-47 fire erupted from the doorway to their right. With no cover to speak of, Doyle and Atticus dropped to the ground and returned fire.

They caught fleeting glimpses of their adversaries as

they poked their heads out the far door to shoot sporadic bursts of undisciplined fire. The two figures were dressed in heavy white winter coats and matching white fur hats, which were oddly out of place in the confines of the grey concrete walls. Not exactly camouflage.

Atticus waited.

Mabel fizzed before dispensing a thick noxious smoke, which enveloped the far end of the entrance hall. Without waiting to be told, Younger Atticus went right, Doyle left. Atticus targeted the door, careful to keep his steps measured and straight amidst the expanding smoke to ensure he was still facing towards the enemy.

Atticus waited.

Random bursts of fire from the Soviets decreased with every advancing step until they stopped completely. The sound of Russian commands combined with coughing fits grew louder.

Atticus continued to wait.

Fighting stinging eyes, he focused on where the doors were. Doyle's smoke bomb had been effective, but its potency soon evaporated. The murky smoke cleared.

Atticus waited.

Slowing his breathing, he kept his finger balanced on the trigger, ready for a target. The smoke dispersed enough to see the white-clad enemy.

Atticus fired.

Two bullets was all it took. Both head shots. Both utterly lethal. The bodies collapsed, rich red spreading across the snow-white camouflage, lifeless eyes wide in shock.

"Greedy bugger, aren't you?" Doyle's words were humorous, but his tone was anything but. "Leave some for the rest of us."

The strain on his face was obvious. A seasoned veteran of countless clandestine infiltrations, this was something else. The sheer violence of the attack was outside the scope of any recorded MI6 operation. Combined with the unknown adversaries still to be faced, this was not what Doyle was accustomed to.

The men passed the threshold and swept for targets. There were none. They turned on their torches. The dark wide concrete hallway was bereft of any signs of life. The same could be said for the next three they traversed down. While the complex was large, the bare fixtures and empty rooms indicated it was barely populated.

Until they reached the room full of computers, that was. By far the largest space they'd encountered, it contained sets of huge mainframe computers, each in a cross formation. There were nine in all. Each had two round screens set into the metal frame with a chunky keyboard below. It was the first time Atticus had seen an actual computer since arriving in this time.

The first one they passed had a label, *CDC 6600*, and had an English keyboard configuration. Every subsequent computer had no such label and had a Cyrillic language keyboard. The purpose of the facility had been confirmed.

With power, the room would no doubt be a noisy cacophony of clanking machinery, cranking out the most basic of digital tasks. As the two walked through the cavern of hulking machines, every computer was silent; it was eerie in the darkened space. The further they traversed, the louder one sound became. It was an odd sound; an ear-splittingly loud version of "Lucille". The men cast a look at one another.

Doyle turned to Atticus. "You don't think Little Richard is actually here, do you?"

"I doubt he's suddenly flipped over to communism and started giving private performances in the middle of Siberia." Atticus frowned. "Probably."

Given how thoroughly Atticus had screwed up time, he couldn't eliminate the possibility entirely. The rendition was so perfect it must have been a recording, though how it was being played when the entire facility was without power was a mystery.

The two stalked their way towards the sound, guns at the ready. Covering each other, they slipped through the large double doorway.

It wasn't entirely what they expected. In fairness, nobody would have expected the scene that lay before them.

Inside was a vast open space with a huge domed roof, roughly the size of a basketball stadium. This must be where the reactor room would have been if the power station had ever been completed. But there was no reactor. Instead, the space resembled an adolescent's fever dream.

Instead of a nuclear reactor and turbines there was an open-plan bedroom, a pool table, a basketball hoop, a table tennis table and several dartboards. There was a smattering of antiques, old books and dusty wine bottles. There were comfortable reading chairs, an open bar and, most comically of all, a hot tub.

Once he rounded a wardrobe, Atticus could see the occupants of the bed. Yes, occupants. Plural.

Careful not to topple any of the numerous bottles of vodka, gin and Coca Cola, Atticus lifted the record needle, silencing Little Richard's rendition of "Good Golly, Miss Molly". The centre resident of the bed sat up.

"What in the name of Kanye West is—?"

It was then Ganim saw the barrel of the submachine gun directed at his head.

Casually he gave a friendly wave. "Oh, hey Atticus. How are things?"

The two other occupants of the bed screeched and pulled the blanket over their buxom frames. A redhead and a brunette. To their credit, they didn't scream, they just stared at Atticus and Doyle in wide-eyed panic.

Doyle lowered his palms slowly, as if to say, *We're not here to harm you.* In return, one of the women gave him a coy little wave.

"I didn't hear you come in." Despite the situation, Ganim managed an almost dignified disposition.

"Did you not hear the explosions?" Atticus shook his head. "The gun fights? We weren't exactly subtle."

"Uh, no." Ganim motioned to his companions. "We were otherwise occupied."

"Aren't you, like, a hundred?" Doyle was gobsmacked.

"Seventy-four, thank you very much," Ganim huffed. "I'm not dead."

"At least not from the waist down apparently." Doyle's gaze bounced between the women.

"How is all this still working?" Atticus pointed to the record player and lights. "We cut the power."

"The electricity here is flaky as fuck, ironic as that is for a nuclear power station, so I generate my own power most of the time."

Atticus flicked his head towards Ganim's companions. "Tell them not to make any loud noises."

In a soothing voice Ganim said, "не волнуйся трактор."

"Your Russian is atrocious." Atticus shook his head.

"I think it's pretty good". Ganim shrugged. "They don't

speak English. I think I'm doing well having only had a brief crash course over the last few months."

"You're really not."

"I am." Ganim was indignant.

Atticus sighed. "What did you just say, then?"

"Don't worry, beautiful."

"Actually, you said, 'don't worry, tractor'."

"I did?" Ganim scratched his stubbled chin.

Still scanning for threats, Younger Atticus asked, "How many internal guards?"

"Just the two." Ganim held up two fingers in case his words weren't indication enough. "They're either patrolling inside or just outside the walls. Boris and Boris. Thick as whale blubber. Not much for conversation either, unfortunately."

"Then you'll be pleased to know that hasn't changed." Atticus tilted his head. "Anyone else?"

"Like who?"

"Like your partner Oliver."

"He's not here and he's not my partner, I assure you. I am but a humble prisoner here."

"If this is a prison," Doyle smiled inanely as he glanced around the well-appointed cavern, "then I'm happy to be locked up."

The women both giggled at Doyle flirtatiously, batting their eyelids. Atticus didn't have the heart to tell them they were barking up the wrong, very tall tree.

Atticus wasn't interested in them either. "There's no one else?"

"No, that's it. Besides Alyona and Sofia here, and they're harmless."

"Harmless?" Atticus smirked. "They're KGB."

Spluttering, Ganim shook his head, perhaps a little too

vehemently. "What? No, they're local girls. Peasants from collective farms nearby. I've taught them a few rudimentary English phrases. They love being here with me. It's like luxury they've never..."

Atticus strode over to the nearest woman and placed the barrel of the Browning to her forehead. "Speak English or I shoot you in the face in three seconds. Three, two..."

"Very well, fine. You got me." Her words held a hint of an accent but she spoke perfect English. "I assume you are Atticus Wolfe, yes?"

"Sofia!" Ganim was aghast. "I've been here for three months and you spoke English the whole time?"

"It saved a lot of needless chit chat, da?" Sofia rolled her eyes. "Although you do love the sound of your own voice, I must say." She turned to Atticus, deadpan. "I assume you'll be killing us now?"

Atticus shook his head. "That's not why we're here." He turned to Doyle. "Find these ladies something to wear, please."

"We can get our own clothes." Alyona's charming smile shone.

"I'm sure you can. But you can just as equally grab a concealed weapon while you're at it. Doyle, if you will."

Doyle complied, rummaging around for some clothing. As he did so, Atticus sat on the end of the bed, his finger resting next to the trigger, just in case. Checking his watch, Atticus huffed. His other self should have been here already. *What's taking him so long?*

Atticus needed to focus on the core mission. "Ganim, what have you told them? More importantly, what have you told Oliver?"

"Nothing." Ganim gulped. "Nothing much."

Atticus frowned and cast him an incredulous look.

"Fine." It appeared Ganim would have dearly loved to tug at his collar, if only he was wearing one. "I gave away very little about the technology itself. Without the keypad, it was a bit redundant anyway, you know? An uphill battle." Seeing that this answer hadn't loosened Atticus's stern face, he stumbled on. "I haven't shared much at all, really. Up until now it was all about my technical requirements. Computational and technical necessities."

If true, that was a relief. It meant removing Ganim from the playing board would take away Oliver's ability to travel in time, rewriting the past, present and future at will. It was also a smart move on Ganim's behalf. Making himself indispensable for as long as possible meant he'd stay alive, and in comfortable surroundings.

Atticus turned to the now-dressed Alyona and Sofia. They both nodded in confirmation.

"Even with our," Alyona placed a hand on her seductive hip, "persuasive methods he gave us nothing about the technical aspects of his work."

Sofia rocked on her heels. "And we are most persuasive."

Alyona went on. "But oh my god, he never shut up about the Liverpool football club. If I live to be a hundred, I hope I never hear about that stupid sport again." She shook her head.

"You said you wanted to hear all about the team..."

She sighed and pointed to her face. "KGB."

Standing, now dressed, Sofia turned to Atticus. "Are you going to kill us now?"

Her tone wasn't desperate, just matter of fact. Very Russian.

"No, I'm not. I want you to send your boss a message. Tell Oliver he lost. He'll continue to lose. Tell him he has one last chance to save his own worthless life. Just stop. Stop trying to change the world. We hold all the cards and he's got nothing left to play. If he stops now, he just might see the real end to the Cold War play out." He checked his watch. "We're about to blow this joint sky high. There are two dead Borises near the entrance, I suggest you take their cold weather gear and start your way back. Don't worry about their weapons, we already removed the firing pins. Off you go. You have ten minutes to get clear before the whole place goes up, and it's a long walk."

Alyona shook her head. "You brought explosives here?"

Doyle grinned. "So, so many."

Atticus pointed back the way they'd come. "Run."

They didn't need to be told twice. The two women sprinted. Ganim watched them go without turning back or offering a word of goodbye. Atticus could virtually hear his geriatric heart breaking. *The old fool.*

Focusing on the conversation at hand, Atticus said, "I saw your computer collection out there. Most impressive."

Still distracted by the sudden and unemotional exit of his companions, Ganim replied, "Ah, yes. I can explain..."

Atticus said nothing, filling the yawning cavern with even more silence.

Realising his answer was insufficient, Ganim turned his full attention to Atticus. "Yes, so, uh the Soviets have been forcing me to develop a time machine for them."

Doyle blinked slowly. "A what now?"

Atticus ignored him. "And you graciously complied."

"They would have killed me!"

Atticus lowered his gaze. "Like I said, you complied." He motioned to the immense room filled with luxuries, perfume still lingering in the air. "And all the while you've been living like the nomenklatura."

"The what?" Ganim's face crinkled in confusion.

"Told you your Russian isn't great. It means the privileged elite."

Ganim shrugged. "If I'm going to be a prisoner, I might as well be a happy one."

Shifting his weight from one foot to the other, Doyle said, "I'm sorry, can we get back to the bit about the time machine?"

Ganim grunted and ignored Doyle. "Fine. I complied. We never got that far, really. They stole the best supercomputer in the world from the Americans and were having a hard time replicating it. They would have got there eventually, but so far most of the work was just installing the big bastards. We've done very little by way of computing the necessary calculations to make it remotely possible. We learned a lot, sure, but I think we were years off even attempting anything resembling a test of any sort, then perhaps another few more before we'd even test a human subject."

Atticus heard the familiar footsteps and glanced up to confirm. "I think you'll find, Ganim, you'll be able to build a device far quicker than that."

Older Atticus came jogging in. He greeted an astounded Ganim with a curt nod.

Younger Atticus went on. "In fact, I'd suggest you'd be ready to send a test subject back in time in less than a year."

Older Atticus was out of breath but managed to give Ganim a cheeky wink.

Younger Atticus briefly took his eyes off the prisoner. "Where have you been?"

Older Atticus raised his eyebrows. "I got lost."

Atticus knew himself. He never got lost. Especially not on a mission.

"Wait a minute." Ganim's jaw dropped lower than the Mariana Trench. "What in the red, white and blue striped bollocks is going on here?" He thrust a finger in Older Atticus's direction. "Are you from the future?"

Older Atticus smiled. "That's a far more complicated question than you could possibly imagine."

Younger Atticus turned to Ganim. "What did you tell Oliver or your faithful companions about what's going to happen in the future?"

"Ah." He tugged his ear, trying to focus, but seemed distracted by the two Atticuses. "Well, I had to give him something, didn't I? He already knew a lot from the book he got off you, he just asked me to fill in some gaps every now and then."

"Every now and then?"

Ganim bobbed his head sheepishly. "Little tidbits. Nothing really."

"Uh-huh. I suggest you start racking your brain to recall *exactly* which gaps you've filled." Atticus cracked his knuckles. "Do you want to get out of here?"

Ganim glanced to where the women had fled. "More than you could possibly know."

"Then get your stuff. Notes, diagrams, anything that's related to your work. Grab everything, because in about ten minutes the rest is going to be cinders." Atticus paused briefly for a second before adding, "Go!"

Ganim scrambled out of bed, got dressed and began rummaging through the stacks of papers.

Younger Atticus filled in his older self what occurred. He didn't press the older man on where he'd been; he knew he wouldn't get an answer. At least not yet. He'd press the subject later.

Watching Ganim scramble about, Older Atticus turned

to his other self. "You think that will make a difference? The message for Oliver?"

"Not in the slightest."

"Then why spare them?"

Atticus wondered why his own self would ask such a question. They weren't cold-blooded murderers. At least, he wasn't. Again, he was left wondering what happened to his other self in the last year.

"Because unlike Oliver, I'm not a sadist who kills for sport."

"You know Oliver's going to keep fucking with the future, right? He's not going to change."

"Oh, I know. In fact, I'm counting on it." Younger Atticus turned to Doyle. "You ready to wipe this place off the map?"

Jolted from the astonished glances he'd been casting between the two Atticuses, Doyle's face lit up.

"Oh, absolutely."

CHAPTER

SIX

A nd wipe it off the map he did. Doyle set the charges, adding anything combustible he could find in the surrounding area, and doused it all in the fuel he'd found in a storage shed. All computer equipment, remaining scientific notes and designs were incinerated in a blast so bright it lit up the surrounding countryside.

A mile away, all five men shielded their eyes. The two Atticuses, Doyle, and a limping Cohen laughed. Beside them stood a bemused Ganim, arms full of folders, rolled-up plans and scant personal belongings. He wasn't anywhere near as amused as the others.

"Jesus, my lad," Cohen shook his head, "you don't do things by halves, do you?"

There was no wiping the proud grin from Doyle's face. Cohen went to work on their escape vehicle. Ganim, seemingly at a loss for what else to do, set about helping him.

Doyle was about to go and help when Younger Atticus grasped his elbow. Older Atticus hung back as well.

"I don't think there's any need to discuss the whole time-machine thing with Cohen, do you?"

Giving a knowing tilt of his head, Doyle said, "I wouldn't even know where to begin."

Older Atticus gave him a thankful pat on the shoulder. "Good man."

"Atticus..." Doyle's tone was tentatively inquisitive, "exactly *when* are you from?"

The Atticuses exchanged looks of concern. This was beyond what they'd wanted to discuss with Doyle.

"Uh, that one's a bit complicated."

"You're from the future, aren't you? Like, a lot of years from now?"

"Okay, so it's not that complicated." Younger Atticus shook his head, impressed. "How the hell did you figure that out?"

"I remember way back you said you were from a place where," he lowered his voice even further, "being a friend of Dorothy was common." He smiled. "You didn't mean a place, you meant..." he shook his head, "you meant the future, didn't you?"

Younger Atticus recalled the conversation they'd had in the car back in Jūrmala, when he'd told Doyle that homosexuality wasn't an issue where he was from. The man had a hell of a memory.

Doyle shook his head. "This is all very HG Wells."

Chuckling, Younger Atticus placed his hand on his shoulder. "It's a lot to take in, I understand. All of this is top secret, of course."

"I completely understand, sir." He squelched his eyes together. "Which is to say, I don't understand any of it, but I'll take it to the grave." His gaze flitted between the two men before him. "And you're really the same person, right?"

Older Atticus nodded. "We are."

"Well," Younger Atticus tilted his head, "he's older. You can tell," he flicked his thumb towards his other self, "by the pudginess."

"I'm not pudgy."

Younger Atticus waved an open hand under his chin and leaned towards Doyle, adding in a conspiratorial stage whisper, "Pudgy."

Chuckling, Doyle went on. "It must be good to know what the other is thinking, able to trust the other person fully. What's that like?"

At the same time, both Atticuses replied, "Complicated."

Doyle wandered off, apparently relieved he wouldn't need to have that particular conversation with Cohen or anyone else for that matter. Younger Atticus glanced at his other self, but didn't share Doyle's relief.

They all went to work on their escape vehicle: another balloon, this one not as large as the last, as they wouldn't be flying over Moscow or other heavily populated areas. They would reuse their flight suits and helmets. They'd bought a spare for Ganim. They only needed to clear Soviet airspace and fly higher than MiGs could safely operate.

As the MI6 agents worked furiously to unfold the equipment from the crate, Atticus watched his older self interacting with the men. Again, he was overcome with a pang of concern. More than concern: dread.

Where exactly had Older Atticus been while they'd been talking to Ganim and the women? He should have arrived the same time they did, even sooner, but instead he arrived late, and panting for breath.

Although Atticus was desperate to ask the man where he'd been, he knew he'd get nothing from him. He could be infuriatingly tight-lipped when he wanted to be. A most annoying trait.

As he watched them unfurl the balloon and prepare the lightweight gondola that would fly them to safety, Atticus had one overwhelming question.

Now more than ever, he wondered what his other self's true agenda really was.

Ganim walked over, sweating from exertion. He motioned to the inflating balloon. "You're not going to push me out of this thing, are you?"

"No." Younger Atticus shook his head before staring Ganim in the eyes. "You broke the world. I'm going to give you the chance to fix it."

~

"MORE CHAMPAGNE, GENTLEMEN?"

"Yes."

"No."

Ganim's head snapped around to Younger Atticus. The pretty young BOAC flight attendant stood behind her trolley, bemused. "So, that's a...?"

"It's a no," Atticus placed Ganim's empty champagne flute on her tray, "but thank you."

She shot him an incandescent smile in return. "Five minutes until take-off, gentlemen. Please ensure your seatbelts are fastened."

Folding his arms with a huff as the attendant bounced away, Ganim mumbled, "Spoilsport."

They sat in the first-class cabin of the 707. The Hong Kong office had managed to secure the entire cabin for their exclusive use on the long-haul flight back to London, in part to rest, in part to use as an interrogation space.

While they waited on the tarmac of the Kai Tak Airport, Cohen slept, Doyle read the local newspaper and Older Atticus played solitaire. Younger Atticus was doing his best to prevent Ganim from becoming too drunk before take-off. They had a lot to discuss, and an inebriated subject wasn't going to give him the answers he sought.

Cohen's leg was in a cast, but he had recovered well. He'd been patched up by medics aboard the aircraft carrier that had picked up their soggy selves in the Sea of Japan. The ship was the *USS Enterprise*. Only Atticus and his other self found that fact amusing.

From there they were transferred to the Royal Navy ship the *HMS Lion* and transported to Hong Kong.

Atticus wasn't sure how long ago they'd lifted off from Siberia, let alone what day it was. He desperately wanted sleep, but he needed answers more.

The plane shunted and taxied. At the end of the runway its engines fired and everyone fell into the usual restlessness before take-off. Ganim gripped the armrests in each hand and grew pale.

On seeing Atticus's reaction he grinned sheepishly. "I'm a nervous flyer."

"Then you're going to love this."

"Love what?"

Atticus was too young to have ever flown out of the infamous Kai Tak Airport but he'd certainly heard about it. It was known as one of the most dangerous airports in the world.

Conveniently situated in the heart of bustling Hong Kong on the Kowloon Peninsula, it was surrounded by tall apartment buildings and mountains on three sides. Pilots had to receive special training before they could fly in and out. Ganim was blissfully unaware of any of these facts.

As the engines roared, the 707 accelerated, pushing the passengers into their seats. The sudden jerk of rapid climb caused Ganim's eyes to flare in alarm. That was before he gazed out the window.

As the plane ascended, it flew between high rises on both sides. They could clearly see into individual apartments at the tips of each wing, residents brushing their teeth and watching television. Ganim's terrified shrieks echoed throughout the plane until they levelled out at 30,000 feet.

When they finally managed to calm Ganim's nerves, he was too highly strung for the interrogation, and besides, everyone else was utterly exhausted. Atticus couldn't recall the last decent sleep he'd had. The few hours in Siberia before the attack on the facility had been restless and on edge. And since the mission was complete they'd been in constant motion, danger all around. It had been as restful as sleeping onstage at a Metallica concert.

They all needed rack time. Sleep first. Ganim wasn't going anywhere. Even before he'd finished the thought, Atticus's eyelids dropped like a closing curtain.

Awoken by a shake of his shoulders, Younger Atticus sat bolt upright and found himself staring into his own eyes.

"It's time. Cohen and Doyle are out."

Yawning, Younger Atticus asked, "Where are we?"

"Over Iran."

"Not usually associated with providing one a sense of safety."

Doyle and Cohen were in the back of the first-class cabin, sleeping soundly. Atticus envied them. He could have slumbered for another two day, but there were more important things than sleep. Ganim was wide awake, as if expecting them. The two Atticuses got into position.

There were two sets of seats on either side of the cabin, so Older Atticus sat across the aisle. It wasn't as intimidating as they'd wanted—Ganim wedged between them—but it would have to do. Younger Atticus ordered a coffee to chase off his lethargy.

"Right." Younger Atticus ran his hands down his thighs. "Let's get on with it. I need you to tell me——"

"How are there two of you?" Ganim checked behind him to ensure Doyle and Cohen were still asleep. It was the first time the three of them had been alone since they'd kidnapped him. "There shouldn't be two of you. What happened?"

Older Atticus spoke up. "Because you helped get me back in time. A year from now, in fact."

"I did? I mean, I do?" Ganim shook his head incredulously. "Why on earth would I do something so unhinged?"

For the next ten minutes Older Atticus explained what had happened to Saigon, almost exactly as he'd explained it to Younger Atticus and Maggie. As he listened to the story, Ganim grew more pallid. By the time Older Atticus told of how he'd materialised in Atticus's flat, Ganim's features were completely washed out.

His face soon hardened. "Just when I thought Atticus Wolfe couldn't fuck things up any worse than you already have, you go and pull this shit." He gestured from one Atticus to the other. "Have you ever considered not doing anything at all? Just laying down for a bit? Every time you try and fix the world you make it infinitely worse."

Younger Atticus refused to take the bait. "Now that we've given you context, we need to know everything you told Oliver. He's hell-bent on changing history, so we need to know exactly what——"

"No."

"No?"

"No." Ganim shook his head.

"No what?"

"I'm not telling you idiots anything until he," he pointed at Older Atticus, "tells me what he's up to." Ganim's eyes narrowed. "He's not telling the whole story. It's obvious he's keeping things from me, and from you lot as well, I suspect. His story has more holes in it than Betty Grable's fishnets."

"I, uh…" Older Atticus stammered. "I don't like what you're insinuating."

"Well I don't like being bullshitted to, so here we are." Ganim folded his arms. "Take for example that only Saigon was bombed. A tragedy, sure, but is that enough for the United Kingdom, who, let's be honest, isn't exactly known for giving two shits about the rest of the world? I'm assuming here that the England funded your time machine because you're not making that shit at home with a transistor radio and a packet of gum."

"They did," Older Atticus conceded.

Ganim shrugged. "Assumed as much. Which gives this bullshit an extra waft of stink. Pick up a history book and virtually all the shitty things that have happened in the world have the UK's grubby little fingerprints all over them. And let's not forget Vietnam isn't even in the Commonwealth. So exactly why would the government expend both money and manpower in the extremely short space of a year to send one man back in time? I'm probably the most qualified person on the planet to tell you the budget and resources required for such an undertaking would be monumental." He shook his head. "I call bullshit."

Younger Atticus found it strange to be in agreement with Ganim. In fact, he found it heartening that he wasn't the only one harbouring doubts about his other self. This went far beyond simply distrusting another man who lusted after the woman he loved.

"If I reveal too much about the future it may disrupt the timeline in all sorts of unknown ways. I can only give you the bare minimum or there could be all sorts of unforeseen consequences."

Growling, Ganim said, "What idiot told you to do that?"

Older Atticus chuckled. "You did."

Unimpressed, Ganim folded his arms. "I'm giving you nothing until he spills his guts." He turned to Older Atticus. "Now let's have it."

"It's complicated."

"That's okay." Younger Atticus settled back in his chair and checked his watch for effect. "We have time."

Older Atticus frowned. "All of a sudden this feels like an interrogation."

Neither Ganim or Younger Atticus argued the point.

"I'm not the bad guy here. If anything, he is." Older Atticus pointed to Ganim. "He was working with the enemy, feeding them god knows what."

"We'll get to that in time." Younger Atticus tried to remain as neutral as possible. "But you have secrets."

"I'm a spy. Comes with the job."

The conversation had certainly pivoted from its original intent but Younger Atticus wasn't about to let the opportunity pass. They were due some answers. It was time for the truth.

"We're finally going to find out what you've been hiding. What you've been keeping from me." Younger Atticus leaned forward. "What really happened before you were sent back in time?"

SEVEN

NINE MONTHS IN THE FUTURE

"Define gone."

"Gone. Gone." The aristocratic toff wheezed in front of the lunchtime tearoom crowd. "Gone."

Rathdowne grunted and put down his cheese sandwich. "I would appreciate it, Vincent, if your vocabulary consisted of more than a singular word. Please elaborate; try speaking like a person who spent more time outside the bar at Cambridge than in it."

"Saigon is gone, sir." Vincent held a torn telex in his hand. "The whole city."

"Did someone pinch it?" Hildebrand-Burke's tone was as indignant as the man himself.

"No." Vincent was white as a sheet. "The Soviets nuked it."

Atticus had never heard a silence like it. It lasted a full

minute before the shock faded and everyone in the room sprinted in all directions. They may have been pompous toffs, but they were dedicated pompous toffs.

Two hours later a dozen of them were crowded in Room 503 poring over whatever scant details they could extract from the region. Reports were flooding in from Tokyo, Hong Kong, Sydney, Kuala Lumpur.

"Details are still coming in." Maggie's usual stoicism had taken a beating in the last few hours. The woman was anxious. They all were. "The Americans think the Reds dropped the Tsar Bomba. Well over fifty megatons. Fifteen times more powerful than Hiroshima."

The room erupted in a chorus of incredulity. Anyone who didn't have a lit cigarette soon did. Maggie went on.

"That's four times bigger than anything the Yanks have right now. It's what they call a planet shaker. The Soviets detonated it in the atmosphere over Saigon, making the devastation all that much worse. The city just isn't there. Any town nearby, gone. And the rest of the country is dead or dying from the radiation. Cambodia is devastated, Malaysia, Singapore, Burma, Philippines, they'll all be receiving fallout by now."

"Jesus."

"The US have five bombers in the air. They've breached Soviet airspace twice already. In response, the USSR scrambled MiGs, but the Yanks had already bugged out, thankfully, so we avoided a shooting war. For five minutes, at least. NATO have put every facility on lockdown alert, recalled all personnel."

Atticus could tell Maggie was struggling to maintain an air of detachment. Just like everyone else.

Rathdowne stood, his fists planted on the tabletop. "Make no mistake, people. We've never been this close to all-out war with a superpower. It's no longer a matter of if now; only when. The Soviets have pulled out of the UN, China's abstaining. Berlin is locked down tighter than a drum. We've just heard there are four divisions of tanks facing off against one another. Berlin will be the first to fall, surely. Austria, West Germany and Finland would be bloody shitting themselves right about now. Both sides are amassing troops on the borders. All our reserves have been called up. There's draft talk already. We're expecting the PM to call a press conference within the hour."

"Why? Why would they do this?"

Pillar voiced the question they all wanted an answer to. Things had certainly escalated in the past few weeks, but this much? Atticus struggled to believe how bad things had become in such a short amount of time. Sure, during the Cold War tensions were always on a knife edge, but for things to escalate so quickly and so horrifically? He could barely keep up.

Maggie had stopped casting him querying glances weeks ago, always silently asking, *did this happen in your time?* By now, she knew the answer. They had deviated so far from the path of history Atticus remembered, they were without a map and heading somewhere dark and deadly.

There was only one explanation for the dire state of the world—Oliver.

After manipulating the Soviet power struggle to put his man Shelepin in charge, things had quickly spiralled out of control. The new hard-line former intelligence officer threw his weight around, exerting his newly acquired status as the head of a superpower.

The target of his plans was Vietnam. Whether at Oliver's behest or as part of his own warped scheme, Shelepin went beyond clandestine support for the North Vietnamese. He deployed Soviet troops on the ground, an event that had never occurred in Atticus's history. Unsurprisingly, US President Johnson pushed back.

It was dick measuring gone mad. No one backed down, and the situation kept escalating until there was way back. The two superpowers seemed determined to turn the Cold War hot.

It was when the US bombed Vladivostok that things really got out of hand. The Soviet city was the key logistics support for North Vietnam. When the CIA informed MI6 the attack was underway two days prior, Maggie had said it was only a matter of time before nukes came into it. How right she was.

Rathdowne wrapped up the meeting and requested that all department heads reconvene at six pm. The rest of those assembled filtered out in a daze. It wasn't every day you realised the Doomsday Clock was about to strike midnight.

Walking down the hall, Maggie and Atticus found themselves alone for the first time since they'd heard the news. Once they rounded a corner, Maggie's hand darted for Atticus's and she gripped it tight.

In a hoarse whisper, she asked, "What can we do?"

"Get in a bunker and pray?"

Evidently this was not the answer she sought. "Where's Ganim?" she asked.

"If he's smart, he'll be in a bunker, praying."

But Ganim wasn't in a bunker. At that moment in time, he was standing in the foyer of the United Kingdom's embassy in Moscow.

Having watched the unfolding events, he had realised as well as they had this was not how history was meant to play out. He saw the world spiralling out of control and headed in only one direction. Whether it was altruistic or self-preservation, or out of the desire for a future to return to, he saw the writing on the wall. The world was ending. Something had to be done.

His nuclear facility had been left virtually defenceless when the guards were recalled to the ever-increasing list of front lines. Ganim had simply walked out the front gate. He'd made his way from Siberia to Moscow via various methods, both legal and illegal.

He'd hitchhiked, begged and bribed his way across three and a half thousand kilometres to the embassy. He arrived dishevelled, his arms laden with scientific notes and diagrams. When he managed to get to the right level of authority, Ganim asked for someone who worked for MI6. Getting him out of Moscow had proven far easier than anyone expected: the entire diplomatic staff were thrown out of the country. He simply went with the wave of personnel, first to Berlin, then to London. While the rest of the world prepared for war, Ganim, Atticus and Maggie set to work trying to prevent it.

IT WAS NOW OFFICIAL. DEFCON 2 had been declared—near nuclear war. It was two days since Saigon and the superpowers were one short step away from a declaring a nuclear war. The 4th Mechanized Brigade of the British Army had been deployed around the Tower of London in order to protect MI6 in a time of war. It hadn't made anyone feel safer.

While everyone at MI6 was in a state of frantic productivity, Ganim, Atticus and Maggie huddled in a small room, working on a plan of their own.

"Too bad we can't design a bomb exclusively for one person," Atticus mused. "The Oliver Bomb has a nice ring to it, don't you think?"

"I think it's too late for that." Ganim frowned out the window at the weather, distracted.

Atticus went on. "We're the only ones who know how messed up events have become. Because you and I know how events *should* have unfolded."

Clearing her throat, Maggie raised her hand. "And you told me, so I'd like to be included, thank you."

"Right you are." Atticus gave her a wink. "The three of us know none of this was meant to happen."

Ganim seemed to concede the point. "True, but none of that helps. We need a solution now."

"Could you replicate the work you were conducting in Siberia?" Atticus attempted to sound as businesslike as possible.

That got all of Ganim's attention. Looking confused, he said tentatively, "I suppose I could, but to what end?" As if on cue, jets flew overhead, rattling the medieval armour.

"Just a theoretical question." *For now,* Atticus didn't add.

"I still have the plans for CDC 6600 from the company in the US." Ganim munched on custard creams, his only request before working. "It's easier than buying one, I guess. Took months before the Soviets got the right parts. Without the keypad, it was an uphill battle, you know?"

"We have the keypad."

"My keypad." Ganim's eyes narrowed.

"*A* keypad." Atticus waited the appropriate amount of time before saying, "We also have a smartphone."

"You what?" Crumbs flew from Ganim's mouth.

"Would that make it easier, in theory?" Atticus couldn't help keep the smirk from his face.

Ganim threw his hands in the air. "Where the fuck was this information months ago?"

Maggie tilted her head. "It was right here, but you were over there."

Ganim's eyes narrowed. "Not by choice."

Waggling her head from side to side, Maggie said, "Sounds like you were pretty comfortable to me."

Ganim had told them he was put up in luxury, with all the food and drink he could want. Reading between the lines, Atticus guessed that meant company as well. All the best scientific minds of the USSR were sent to assist him, and any equipment he requested would arrive the next day. He wanted for nothing.

"But even with everything I asked for I was unable to get anywhere near the computing power needed, let alone a functioning test machine. I don't know if we ever would, to be honest. Maybe after a decade?" He shrugged. "Not that I was motivated."

"What about now?" Atticus pointed to the newspaper on the table before them. The headline read, "The End?" with an accompanying picture of a mushroom cloud over what was once Saigon. Atticus extracted the keypad and his time apocryphal mobile phone and placed them before Ganim. "Now you have access to the computational power of a device decades more advanced than anything on the planet. You could use this to continue your research, couldn't you?"

"Hypothetically it's possible, but..." Ganim shook his head, "I ask again, to what end?"

Maggie turned to Atticus, equally lost.

91

"What if we built a time machine for someone to go back in time and undo what Oliver has done?"

Both Maggie and Ganim regarded him as if he were mad. Perhaps he was.

Ganim took his time answering. "In case you missed it, the world is about to go to hell. Like I said, the Soviets were a decade away from cracking the first step towards time travel, even with my brilliance."

Atticus ignored the arrogance. "Yes, but you also said you weren't motivated." He pointed at the front page of the newspaper. "What about now? You have all the research your brilliant mind conceived, all the technical diagrams showing how to make it work with current technology. Plus, now you have the keypad and a mobile phone." He tapped them for effect. "You have everything you could possibly need. What if you could send someone back in time to stop Vietnam from being wiped off the map? To save millions, likely billions of lives? Wouldn't that be worth it?"

"What you're suggesting would take an unparalleled commitment, an unprecedented—"

"Can it be done?"

Ganim stared Atticus in the eye, a glimmer of hope shining for the first time. "Yes." His eyes narrowed. "I believe it can. Yes."

"Well, let's get fucking started then."

FOR A FEW WEEKS the global situation eased. The world was stricken by a sudden and inexplicable desire to not die horribly at the base of a mushroom cloud. However, most suspected the rational cessation of hostilities would only be fleeting. Declarations of war hadn't been issued, but that seemed due to logistical reasons rather than political ones. You could smell war in the air. The world apparently wasn't ready to push itself over the precipice into mutually assured destruction. Not yet. But few believed the uneasy armistice would hold.

Predictably, the diplomatic situation grew worse. An F-4 Phantom downed a MiG-21 over the Sea of Japan. On the border between East and West Germany, two divisions of tanks engaged in open warfare. The Gulf of Aden was mined, taking out two Iranian tankers before all oil shipments were halted. Soviet troops crossed the border and invaded Norway before retreating hours later. The First Secretary of Czechoslovakia was publicly and violently thrown out of office—and there were rumours he was then quietly executed—for speaking out against the escalating warmongering.

Rathdowne, through Atticus, convinced the government that Ganim was developing a super weapon. A computer program able to track intercontinental missile launches, as well as improve the efficiency of the UK's nuclear arsenal under the auspices of the Strategic Air Command. The government threw truckloads of money at it.

Ganim tinkered and toiled. In spite of the growing world crisis, Atticus grew to like working with him. Maggie too.

Oliver was spotted at the May Day march, ominously close to Alexander Shelepin, the brand-new head of the Soviet Union. The two KGB buddies stood close on the podium as they watched the Soviet machine march to the drum of war. The two had been instrumental in ousting the previous leader, Brezhnev, after only a few months in power.

The Soviets, now with Chinese backing, rattled their sabres. Ultimatums were issued. The Allies had one week to remove themselves from Berlin. If not, Washington would follow Saigon straight to hell.

Governments the world over told everyone to build bunkers. Panic struck. Supermarkets were stripped of every morsel of food. It was a million times worse than the early Covid-19 panic of Atticus's day. Looting, riots. The world went mad.

That's when they knew for sure they had to send someone back, while they still could. They had to try and wind back the madness. Save the world. If they took too long, London would be a pile of ash and there would be no one left to send back. They had to act.

It was ten o'clock at night. Atticus, Maggie and Ganim sat exhausted around an empty wooden packing box, their makeshift dinner table. They were too spent to go home.

In the face of their fatigue, Atticus and Maggie still held hands. Ganim noticed and gave the couple a genuine smile, albeit a tired one. The three ate their ration packs in silence, unable to unhook from their work, a million details circulating in their brains.

"When do you think you can send me back?"

Maggie sat bolt upright, suddenly alert. She glared at Atticus. "You?"

Atticus shook his head in confusion. "That was always the intent," he turned to Ganim, "wasn't it?"

It was clear from Maggie's reddening face Atticus may have misjudged the group's assumptions.

"Like hell it was."

Atticus sat up. "Wait, who did you think we were going to send?"

"Anyone else!" Maggie's arms flailed. "Someone single. Someone who was fine with it being a one-way ticket."

"But...but..." Atticus had to choose his words carefully to avoid inflaming the situation further. "It has to be me, surely you can see that? Who else can persuade those that need convincing? Who else knows what's at stake? Who else knows Oliver? It has to be me. I thought it was obvious."

In retrospect, his word choice was less than stellar.

"It wasn't obvious! Does my face look like it was fucking obvious?"

Maggie stormed out, slamming the door behind her for good measure. Atticus went to go after her, but Ganim held his arm and shook his head.

"Let her go, son. For a little bit, at least. She's going to need some time."

"She will, will she? How the hell would you know that?"

Ganim shook his weathered head. "You might be a good spy, Atticus Wolfe, but you have a lot to learn about women."

"Am I wrong, though? I'm the only one who can go back."

Shaking his head once more, Ganim said, "That's my point. It doesn't matter if you're right or not. In love, being right is irrelevant."

"And what is relevant, then?"

With a groan that sounded like it came from the depths of Ganim's seventy-four years, he said, "The fact that you have to ask shows you don't have the answer."

"But... that's how questions work."

"That woman loves you, down to her very bones, the

poor thing. It doesn't matter if you're literally saving the world, which you would be. All that matters right now is that you'll be leaving her. And that's the one thing that terrifies her more than losing the world: losing *you*. When it boils down to it, that's precisely what it's about, son. She loves you more than the entire world. The fact that you didn't see it means you're a bigger idiot than I gave you credit for."

"Thanks very much." Atticus scratched the back of his head. "I'm going to..." He flicked his thumb towards the door.

"Go on then," Ganim gave him a knowing grin. "Try and be less of an idiot this time if you can."

"I make no promises."

Atticus found Maggie in the makeshift tea room on the second floor. She sat on a hard wooden chair, her legs tucked under her chin. It was plain she'd been crying. In Atticus's experience, that was a rarity.

She spoke without glancing up. "I know you're right, but that doesn't mean you're not a giant twat."

"But I'm not right, about a great many things."

That caused her to look up. Atticus realised the next few words were perhaps the most important of his life.

"I love you, Maggie Dunbar. You've heard me say those words a million times, and I've meant it every time, with every fibre of who I am. I'm not doing this for the sake of the world. It's not altruism; it's the opposite, in fact. I'm doing this because of my love for you. Going back in time means we'll have a chance of a life together. If not us, a different version of us. It's pure selfishness. I want to give another version of me the chance to live an eternity with the woman he loves more than life itself. That's why. Because for the first time in my life, I have something worth living for. Someone I'll risk everything for. And to be absolutely clear, that person is you, Maggie, and the other person is me, the giant twat."

Atticus knew his words had an effect. There was the slightest shadow of a smirk. The faintest humorous squint of her eyes.

"Curse you and your smooth ways, Atticus Cornelius Wolfe."

"That's not my middle name."

She crinkled her nose. "It is now."

"You said you liked my smoothness."

"Oh, I do, but it can be damned annoying when I'm mad at you."

"I can imagine."

"I always knew it was going to be you," she said, darkness returning to her features. "I just never wanted think about it because that would make it real. If I brought it up, gave it oxygen, I knew you'd confirm it. So I pretended it wasn't a thing. Ignorance is bliss and all."

For the first time in minutes, Atticus breathed again.

Gaze wandering off into the middle distance, Maggie slyly said, "But I have been thinking..."

"Oh no. Just when I thought I was out."

"Shh, this is actually important."

"Unlike the fate of the world?"

"Right." She straightened her back. "We've been seeing each other for nearly a year now."

Atticus fought to keep his voice from slipping into a higher octave. "Yes."

"I don't know about you, but where I come from, *when* I come from, that usually means something."

"An anniversary dinner?" Atticus was fully aware of the extent to which he was clutching at straws.

Maggie glared. "Marriage."

"Oh."

Dating in the sixties was far more structured than in his day. The fact that they called it courting just made it more antiquated. People didn't date multiple partners for years, possibly decades, as in Atticus's time. Once you found a partner who wasn't thoroughly awful, couples tended to marry early. Even after a few months of Maggie and Atticus dating, her friends had started hinting at marriage. Atticus had assumed the two of them would eventually get married, but thought it would be several years before they had this particular conversation. As he had been about many things recently, he was wrong.

Breaking eye contact, Maggie glanced down and wrung her hands. "But you're always so keen to disappear. Into the future, and now into the past. If I could talk about that with Mary I'm sure she'd tell me I'm wasting my time with you."

"Your best friend can be blunt, true."

"But she's bloody perceptive sometimes, too." Maggie let out a tiny laugh. "I was going to ask if we had a future, Atticus, but that's a way more complicated question with you, isn't it?"

Leaning down, Atticus took Maggie's hand. "When we get through this—and we will, together—you'll get the proposal you deserve, Maggie. That, I promise you."

Her face brightened, but there was sadness in her eyes. "Don't make promises you can't keep."

"I will tear this world down to get to you, Maggie Dunbar. Nothing's going to stop me from keeping my word."

"Not even the end of the world?"

"Not even the end of the world."

They kissed and Atticus wondered if he had enough funds saved up for a ring.

He felt an emotion he hadn't felt in so long he initially had trouble identifying it. Hope.

He should have known better. The next morning everything changed.

"The Reds have just crossed the border into Norway." Rathdowne gazed up from his morning briefing report. "They faced little opposition. They're not retreating this time. They're charging through the country like last yesterday's curry."

"Jesus."

Atticus kicked himself for his momentary optimism. He looked over at Maggie; there was real fear in her eyes now. An invasion of another country was not an undertaking to secure peace. There was only one way this would end.

Rathdowne went on. "At the head of the convoy were twenty-two ICBMs. What that means, lady and gentlemen, is that when they get to the tip of Norway on Thursday afternoon the Soviets can spit on Aberdeen if they choose to. They can also stick a missile up the hallway of Balmoral before we even know it's launched. This is it, people. We're at end game now." He turned to Ganim. "Please tell me you're close to cracking this thing because we have no other options left."

BACK TO NINE MONTHS BEFORE

"WITH THE MOTIVATION of nuclear missiles at our doorstep and an Asian capital city lying in radioactive cinders," Older Atticus took a breath and continued, "Ganim and his team were successful in creating a functional time machine to send me back here. And the rest you know."

Ganim and Younger Atticus stared at Older Atticus with what could be classified as incredulous looks on their faces. The plane tilted slightly and its airspeed reduced.

Younger Atticus leaned forward. "Your tale, uh," he turned to Ganim for confirmation, "ended rather abruptly there. Saigon gets wiped out, Ganim makes his way to London, you get to work and then...?"

Ganim raised an agreeing eyebrow. He'd been thinking the same thing.

"There's a huge chunk of the story that's missing." Younger Atticus clenched and unclenched his fists. "It's like, oh, Jesus was born and anyway, he got nailed to a thing."

Absentmindedly, Ganim looked up. "That's kind of the Bible though, isn't it? He's born and then thirty years later oh hey, listen to this." On seeing blank expressions from both Atticuses, he added, "The lost years? Didn't you blokes ever go to Sunday school? I'm the non-Christian and even I know that."

"No," Older Atticus replied, seeming pleased to be talking about something else. "Our father was either getting us to steal stuff while others were at church or to bail him out of jail for whatever he did the night before."

For a fleeting second Younger Atticus wondered about his family in Brixton, how his beloved grandmother was getting on. But that's all it was: fleeting. There were more important things.

He went on. "I can't help but think there's more to the story."

"Like what?" If Older Atticus was trying for the sincerity of a real estate agent, he pulled it off admirably.

"Like," Ganim's voice was close to a screech before he calmed his tone, "what else happened around the world, who was attacked and... and..." the agitated septuagenarian waggled his hand at the Older Atticus, "and not least why you were wearing a Soviet uniform!"

Countering the excited Ganim, Younger Atticus attempted to remain calm. Or at least, calm*er*. "There's missing parts to your story, is what we're saying. It ended very abruptly."

"This seems very intimate."

All three sets of eyes turned to Cohen, who rested his chin on the seat behind Ganim. They all stopped abruptly, wondering the same thing. *What had he heard?*

"How's the leg?" Older Atticus asked across the aisle.

"Still attached, so I'm counting that as a win." He gave everyone a cheeky grin followed by a yawn. "What are you blokes bollocking on about? You're all very serious, so it's either work or women." He shuffled around the seat and sat next to Older Atticus. "You're in luck, because I'm an expert at both."

"Work."

"Women."

Ganim and Younger Atticus exchanged glances, having answered at the same time. Older Atticus sat in square-jawed silence.

"Working women?" Cohen chuckled. "My favourite kind. Did I ever tell you blokes about the time—"

"Ladies and gentlemen, as we start our descent into Heathrow, please make sure your seat backs and tray tables are in their full upright position..."

All members of the first class instinctively looked up

and waited for the pilot's announcement to conclude. Doyle wandered over and gave everyone a wave of greeting while they waited for it to end.

"Please make sure your seat belt is securely fastened and all luggage is stowed appropriately. Thank you."

Younger Atticus cast his counterpart a look. Knowing the recipient as well as he did, he hoped the message was received loud and clear.

This isn't over. I'll get that missing piece of the story one way or another. And whatever else you're hiding.

CHAPTER

EIGHT

Younger Atticus needed a coffee. Shame there was none to be had.

He still found it odd that he could walk to work and not pass a single shop selling a takeaway coffee. The very concept was completely foreign to contemporary Londoners. In Atticus's day you couldn't throw a reusable cup without hitting a coffee shop. The closer you were to the centre of London, the better the ratio became, until virtually every second shop was feeding London's caffeine addiction.

The Younger Atticus missed his local café, Kanga Brew, which he'd popped into every day on his way to work. He forged on, craving the bitter treat that was still decades away from becoming the norm.

In spite of the lack of caffeine, Atticus and Maggie had picked up Ganim from his safe house and escorted him to the new MI6 offices. All three passed the multiple security checks and stepped behind the walls of the imposing fortress. Atticus still found it odd that he worked in the Tower of London.

As they strode past the subtly named Bloody Tower, Atticus wondered about MI6's future. In his time, MI6 had moved location in the nineties after Century House was designated "irredeemably insecure" by the National Audit Office. But now that Century House had been destroyed, a new home would have to be found far sooner than that. Atticus pondered if in years to come MI6 would relocate to Vauxhall Cross, or to somewhere else entirely.

He really had made a mess of the timeline.

Striding around the grounds, Ganim was visibly anxious. It may have been the majesty of the surrounds or, just as likely, the security. Perhaps both. Maggie found his sense of awe pleasantly amusing.

As far as the public were concerned, no one had been apprehended for the bombing of MI6 headquarters. All sorts of wild speculation had been bandied about in the press, from the KGB to Irish Republicans to MI6 itself in an attempt to receive greater funding. Of course, none had identified the real culprit.

It was Mikhail, Oliver's henchman, who had planted the bomb at Century House. Oliver, the newly ordained Soviet citizen, had quickly and mercilessly used the bombing as an excuse to pave the road of his ascension. He'd manufactured evidence that rogue KGB elements had executed the attack, coincidentally the very same men who stood in his way of seizing more power. Senior Soviet intelligence officers had suddenly disappeared and hadn't been seen again. Oliver certainly was ruthless in his efficiency.

Maggie pointed out the ancient building that held their office to Ganim. Atticus wondered if his older self would be inside. He'd peeled off once they'd cleared customs, and hadn't returned to Atticus's flat. That only fuelled his suspicions.

Maggie opened the door to the White Tower and all three took to the stairs, clomping up the heavy wooden staircase to the third floor.

"I have only one question." Maggie's cheerful voice ascended the stairs ahead of them. "If we get this time machine of yours working, can we...", she left a cheeky pause, "... travel forward in time to know who wins the Grand National?"

"No." Ganim straightened his back in alarm.

"Okay, so no Grand National then." Maggie nodded her head and took a couple of steps before turning back. "So, follow-up question—"

"You mean after the one question you were going to ask?" Atticus smirked.

"Yes." She poked him good-naturedly in the ribs. "Can we travel forwards to grab a really successful book, call it our own and make squillions?"

"No." Ganim didn't seem to find this line of questioning as amusing as Atticus did. "Not only would that be immoral, we can't risk all the unforeseen consequences that may arise because of it."

Maggie nodded again studiously. "Another question."

Atticus chuckled. "This is really stretching the definition of one."

"Can we kill Hitler?"

Atticus and Ganim stopped dead in their tracks and peered up at Maggie standing serenely on the stairs before them.

"Wait, what?" All of a sudden Atticus was less amused.

"Hitler. Can we kill him?" Maggie's face was as neutral as if she'd asked what the weather was going to be today.

"Why? No, scratch that, we all know why." Atticus scowled. "But *why* why?"

Waggling a finger at him, Maggie said, "And you complain about my numbering system."

"Because we don't know what would happen if we did kill Hitler." Ganim spluttered.

"You mean something bad?"

"Yes!"

"Worse than Hitler?"

"Potentially," Ganim nodded, "yes."

Maggie placed her hands on her hips. "Name one thing worse than Hitler."

"Phil Collins."

Ganim gave Atticus an approving frown. "I'm not going to disagree with that. I fucking hate 'Easy Lover'. Shits me to tears." He sighed deeply. "To be honest, as much as I want to get back to my time, I don't know if it's wise to create another time machine. I believe we need to focus on the one thing we've been tasked to do: stop this Oliver chap and the mess you've made of the timeline."

Maggie and Atticus weren't about to argue with that. If they failed, there would be no need to worry about where MI6 would be located. Or Phil Collins, for that matter. London, MI6 and every city around the globe could be wiped off the map.

"There's only one mission here." Ganim's voice was grave. "Everything else will have to wait." He squinted. "Including any discussions about killing Hitler. Make no mistake, the future we knew," he pointed at Atticus," doesn't exist. If somehow we fix this shitshow you've created, then we can talk about the potential of one time trip only. And that's back home and getting out of history's way."

Atticus shot Maggie a glance. They still hadn't had *that* conversation.

Ganim went on, oblivious to their exchange. "How well we repair the damage already done will determine whether the place we return to even resembles the one we remember. Who knows, England might even be good at football, or Eurovision, or... anything, really." He exhaled loudly. "Maybe we could get back and find out, I don't know. We have to right things first, though."

As they continued ascending the stairs, the occasional glance between Atticus and Maggie conveyed an unspoken discussion. *We need to talk.*

The old man shook his head as they passed the second floor. "Imagine going back to our time and not knowing what was going to happen. Imagine that!" He shook his head gleefully. "You wouldn't know how society's going to turn out, which song will be a hit and which one won't. Oh, to have a sense of wonder again."

While Ganim was taken by a sense of whimsy, Atticus was feeling far less fanciful. They made their way to their office, settled in and got Ganim working on a theoretical wish list of what he would need to build a time machine.

"Maggie, we've got a debrief in ten." Atticus jerked his head towards the door. "Shall we?"

Though Maggie bobbed her head in agreement, it was clear her thoughts were elsewhere. They bid Ganim farewell and headed back down the stairway. Halfway down, Atticus stopped dead and turned to Maggie.

"I don't want to go back to my own time."

"I..." Maggie blinked several times as she processed the words. "Are you... are you sure?"

Atticus broke into a grin. "I really am. It feels wonderful to say it out loud. Let me try again." He cleared his throat. "I don't want to go back to the twenty-first century. Yep. Feels amazing."

Maggie leapt into his arms and kissed him. "I bloody love you."

"I bloody love you."

He kissed her back for good measure.

Tucking a stray hair behind her ear, he said, "And before you ask again, yes, I'm really sure. I've been meaning to say it for ages, but, you know..."

"Homicidal mole agents, getting chucked out of MI6, gangsters, fights with the KGB, getting back into MI6, clandestine extraction missions to Siberia to save the future? That kind of thing?"

Atticus took Maggie's hand. "But none of that means anything if I can't be with you."

Gently extracting her hand from his, Maggie placed her hands either side of Atticus's face. "With a line like that I don't know whether to kiss you or slap you."

"What, why?"

"Oh my god it was corny as hell, but fucking sweet." She kissed him, hard. "You're lucky you're pretty."

"I'm... not entirely sure what's happening here..."

For good measure, Maggie kissed him again. "Oh, you're good, cowboy, believe me. You're good." She gave him a cheeky wink. "Come on, we've got a meeting." She took out her lipstick. Between applications she said, "We need this day to be over so we can get to tonight that much faster."

"Why, what's happening tonight?"

Maggie cast him an expression as if in that moment he was the stupidest man alive. He may very well have been.

THEY EVENTUALLY FOUND OLDER ATTICUS. He was sitting in Rathdowne's office.

Unable to continue the questioning from the flight or ask where he'd spent the night, Younger Atticus sat next to his other self silently, their only exchange a curt nod. Older Atticus's beard was beginning to come into its own. It was getting easier to tell the two apart.

Ganim came into the office timidly, as if expecting to be arrested at any moment. As far as Atticus knew, Ganim hadn't broken any laws in this timeline. As far as he knew.

It took a moment, but when Ganim realised there were two Atticuses in the same room as a senior MI6 official his complexion became even more pallid.

Once Maggie took her seat, Rathdowne observed the assembled bodies from the other side of his desk.

"Well, that was a cock-up, wasn't it?"

"I think if you read the report—"

"Oh, I've read the report. I'm considering renaming it The Report on Operation Cock-up."

"We were successful in our mission." Younger Atticus motioned towards Ganim. "That's the main point, isn't it? I would have thought that was enough?"

"Not when you blow up half of Northern Asia in the process. No, Mr Wolfe, I wouldn't consider that enough. You're just lucky nobody's kicked up a stink about it." He frowned like only Rathdowne could. "That either means the Kremlin want to keep your smash and grab under wraps until the right time, or—"

"Or this was so off the books they didn't even know about it?"

Rathdowne gave Maggie an approving tilt of his head. "Exactly, Miss Dunbar. Given the nature of the traitorous weasel behind all this, I'm leaning towards the latter."

Rathdowne turned to the pasty Ganim and folded his hands before him. "I've yet to hear from the man himself. So tell me, Omar Ganim, what did you tell Oliver Preston about the future?"

In response, Ganim's mouth constricted. He spun to face Younger Atticus. "He *knows*?"

Nodding, Younger Atticus replied, "He does. About you, me, him," he flicked a thumb at his other self. "It became important for him to know about everything. We'd never have gained approval for the mission to Siberia without him knowing the whole story and what was at stake."

"Was that a compliment, Wolfe?"

"Just a statement of fact, sir."

Rathdowne lifted an eyebrow. "And I don't think you've called me sir before, either. Are you feeling well? Need a lie down?" Turning his attention back to Ganim, Rathdowne put on an expectant expression. "Well?"

"I, uh, didn't tell him anything?"

A wall of indignancy stared back at Ganim.

He coughed. "Well, next to nothing."

No one else in the room spoke.

"Alright fine. It was mostly about football." He shifted uncomfortably in his seat. "But also, er, how the Cold War turned out."

Younger Atticus threw his arms up and grunted.

"He already knew!" Ganim's voice grew higher. "He said he had a book on how the Soviet Union lost, describing their downfall in great detail. He already had all the information. Brezhnev, stagnation, Reagan, everything. All he asked me was how people felt about it. What it was like to grow up with the threat of the big bad Soviets, did everyone really hate them, that sort of thing."

Rathdowne placed his forefingers to his lips, taking in

this information. "I suppose the next question is, are you going to build us a time machine?"

"Excuse me?" Ganim's voice broke. "I thought it was all theoretical at this point? What does MI6 want with a time machine?"

"I don't bloody want one." There was disdain in Rathdowne's voice. "But we need it as backup in case the mess he's made," his palm swung between the two Atticuses, "gets any worse." He extracted a handkerchief from his pocked and wiped the sweat from his brow. "And by worse, I mean nuclear bombs detonating over capital cities, in case that was unclear." He shook his head as he muttered to himself, "My life used to be so simple."

Raising a hand as if he were in a classroom, Ganim appeared alarmed. "Um, backup? As I understand it, we have only a few months. From what he said," he motioned to Older Atticus, "it took a substantial investment and a sizable chunk of the national budget to pull it all together and that was only after Saigon was obliterated and the likelihood of a nuclear winter became a reality." He shook his head. "I'm only one man. Without assistance it will take me literally years using current technologies, possibly decades."

"Would this help?"

From his jacket pocket, Older Atticus extracted a wad of papers. He unfolded the pages and handed them to Ganim.

"What's this then?" Ganim's eyes flew open and he flicked through the pages rapidly. His head jerked up and he stared at Older Atticus in amazement. "Is this...?"

"The final plans of a working time machine?" There was no hiding the glee on Older Atticus's face. "Your future self thought you might find them handy. It uses everything available in this timeline—the phone, the keypad, present-day computers—and, more importantly, tells you how to program them to get it all working." He pointed at the papers. "As you can see, it's all there. All it needs is your brilliance to put it together."

Younger Atticus stood in alarm. "Why the hell wouldn't you tell us you had this as soon as you arrived? Why would you keep this a secret?"

"Because I'm a spy." Older Atticus shrugged. "Keeping secrets is what we do."

Younger Atticus crossed his arms. "That's an evasive answer and you know it."

Older Atticus pointed to his face and in a low whisper said, "Spy."

"You've been keeping shit secret from yourself." Younger Atticus shook his head. "You've been lying to yourself."

Older Atticus splayed his palms, serene as a Buddhist monk. "In a way, aren't we all lying to ourselves?" Seeing the incoming tirade from his younger self, he put up a hand. "I was advised just before I left not to reveal anything apart from the bare essentials. The *bare essentials*. Anything more could jeopardise everything."

"What idiot told you that?" Ganim folded his arms.

Older Atticus smirked. "You did."

Arms unfolded, amusement danced on Ganim's lips. Maggie's too. But not everyone was falling for Older Atticus's charm.

"I still don't buy it." Younger Atticus clenched his fists. "You're deliberately—"

"Alright." Rathdowne clapped his hands together. "We don't have time to get in the middle of a lovers' tiff, or whatever the hell this is. Sit." He glared at Younger Atticus until he complied. "We've got a lot to discuss, all of it more important than who knew what, when. And you," he pointed to Ganim, "review that and tell me what you need."

Still immersed in the paperwork, written in his own handwriting, Ganim nodded. "I will. This cuts down development time considerably." He let out a huge sigh. "By years, in fact. This is doable." He glanced up. "This is very doable."

It was as close as Rathdowne ever got to being pleased. He moved on. "The main game now is stopping Preston."

Maggie sat up. "While everyone else was gallivanting around the USSR," she gave Younger Atticus a good-natured frown, no doubt trying to calm his obvious temper, "I've been working on a psychological profile of Oliver. Determining the best way to divert him from his path. I've run some scenarios—"

"Scenarios?" Rathdowne seemed lost.

"Scenarios, yes, against his personality type."

"Psychopath, you mean?"

"More sociopath, actually." Maggie wriggled in her chair, making herself comfortable, as if she'd been waiting for this moment. "Psychopaths are people who have little or no conscience. Sociopaths, on the other hand, do have a limited, albeit weak, ability to feel empathy and remorse. Psychopaths can follow social conventions when it suits their needs. Sociopaths are more likely to fly off the handle and react violently whenever they're confronted by the consequences of their actions. That's Oliver to a tee." She turned to Younger Atticus. "Especially when it comes to Atticus. He feels things passionately, not dispassionately, like a psychopath." Maggie repositioned herself again. "Whether he knows it or not, Oliver is obsessed with Atticus. His wildest actions seem to occur when Atticus is involved. We can potentially use that to our advantage."

Rathdowne chortled. "You make it almost sound like the bloke is in love with him."

Straight-faced, Maggie replied, "I believe he is, yes."

"In love? With a... man?" Rathdowne went to laugh until he realised no one else was amused. "But he's not a," Rathdowne let his wrist go limp, "... is he?"

Everyone else in the room did their best to ignore the homophobia. For Atticus, this was one of the most disconcerting aspects of living in the sixties. Homosexuality was still a criminal offence. The only public portrayals were offensive, mincing caricatures played for laughs. As far as Atticus was concerned, Oliver's sexual orientation was irrelevant; unlike the consequences of obsession.

Maggie picked up her thoughts. "Oliver's infatuation runs deep. Probably deeper than even he realises. Using various profiling techniques, we can build up some scenarios we can use."

Rathdowne picked up a cigarette, likely using the time to compose himself and mull over what Maggie had just said. "So your scenarios, you think these could potentially be used to dissuade him from..."

"Destroying the planet and leaving nothing alive bar the cockroaches? Yes, I do."

Atticus was impressed. Maggie had shown an aptitude for psychological profiling when they were in Latvia. It was clear she'd run with it. He shot her an approving glance.

Taking a moment to puff on his cigarette, Rathdowne scowled as if he'd come to a conclusion. "Right. Pack your bags, you two. You're off to Moscow."

"Now?"

Frowning, Rathdowne replied, "Yes, Miss Dunbar, unless you have a more pressing engagement?" Without waiting for an answer, he pressed on. "I don't believe this can wait. Your target is Oliver Preston. You'll have IDs, tickets and papers on your desk within the hour. I doubt we'll get you on a flight tonight, so you'll ship out tomorrow."

"Good." There was relief in Maggie's tone.

Rathdowne raised another eyebrow. "Do you have something on tonight?"

"I won't, no."

It took all Younger Atticus's strength not to react to that. He skewed his mouth to one side to cover his smirk. Older Atticus positively bristled at the exchange.

"What exactly will they be doing in Moscow?" Older Atticus's question was gruff, verging on harsh.

To Younger Atticus, he appeared agitated, though he was unsure if it was the playful banter he'd exchanged with Maggie or something else. Possibly both.

Rathdowne clasped his hands together. "Find Preston, if they can, and talk some sense into him. Tell him if he stays on the course he's on he'll be responsible for sending half of Asia radioactive."

"They need to kill him."

All heads spun to Older Atticus.

"He's not Hitler." Maggie cast an eye to Younger Atticus, harking back to their previous conversation. "He's super intelligent. He may have moments of being unhinged, but he can still be reasoned with. We can get through to him if we appeal to his—"

"You need to kill him." There was a tenor of anger in Older Atticus's words. "No talk. No mercy. Just kill the bastard." He made a gun with his fingers. "One shot. Bang. In the head. That will stop all of this."

"This may come as a shock, but MI6 is not in the habit of carrying out assassinations." In contrast to Older Atticus,

Rathdowne's words were calm and unhurried. "If that changes, I'll let you know."

"We're not talking about a simple murderer here. He's the most dangerous man on the planet. Oliver is too dangerous to be on the loose. He's too dangerous to live."

Rathdowne's tone was that of a kindly school teacher explaining a rudimentary fact. "Perhaps. But what if he's shared the history book with others? Or put in motion contingencies for his sudden and unexpected demise? Hell, he could have made arrangements to launch every single Soviet nuke should his heart stop for all we know." Rathdowne shook his head. "No, we talk first and take it from there."

Younger Atticus could virtually hear his older self stewing in his own juices. It wasn't what he wanted to hear, but he understood Rathdowne enough to know he wouldn't be swayed once his mind had been made up.

Younger Atticus thought it best to move on. "What about..." he tilted his head towards the other Atticus. He still had plenty to discuss with the other version of himself. First and foremost, the rest of the story about how he arrived in this time, and secondly, why he had withheld the fact he possessed plans to build a functioning time machine. And thirdly and most recently, why he was so hell bent on killing Oliver. The passion he exhibited about killing their nemesis was fervent to the point of mania.

"You'll be operating as two teams. The younger Wolfe is off to Moscow to stop Preston." He turned to Older Atticus and added, "By *talking* to him, and without the aid of bullets preferably. The older Wolfe stays with Ganim, because he's the most likely to shed any light on whatever he picked up during the rapid development of the time machine."

It was a logical plan, it was just one Younger Atticus wasn't entirely comfortable with. The meeting broke up and the two teams split off. Ganim was to operate from a makeshift laboratory on the first floor. He and Older Atticus would be given on-site accommodation within the Tower of London's compound. Ganim was seemingly indifferent to being held a virtual prisoner; it wouldn't be his first time. It also meant Older Atticus could easily avoid his other self before they left for Moscow.

On the way back to their office, Maggie touched Younger Atticus's arm. "What's up?"

"He's being deceitful."

"Who? The other you?"

"I just don't trust him."

Maggie gave a concerned chuckle. "You don't trust yourself?"

He held her gaze. "Why was he so gung ho about killing Oliver? His story is incomplete. The man's hiding something. A lot of somethings."

Maggie looped her arm through his. "Wow. An Atticus Wolfe who's mysterious. I wonder what that's like?"

Atticus glanced out the window to see Older Atticus and Ganim making their way across the grounds to the Yeoman Warders living quarters.

"You know what I mean."

"I do. But we have bigger things to worry about than your trust issues." There was sympathy in Maggie's eyes, but mostly determination. "What if we fail? Let's be honest, our track record of success is pretty light on. Rathdowne's right, we need the contingency those two can give us. We need Ganim and the other you working on the time machine. If we fail, we're going to have to go back, maybe even further. But we won't let that happen, will we? We're going to stop Oliver, right?"

Atticus watched his other self disappear at the opposite end of the grounds. Maggie was absolutely right, that should be their focus. Whatever Older Atticus was hiding could wait.

"Absolutely." Atticus tapped the window frame with his fingers. "We need to do whatever it takes to ensure Leonid Brezhnev keeps the leadership and Oliver's buddy Shelepin is kept out. Everything spiralled out of control as soon as he took the reins. They have to be stopped." He turned to Maggie. "Everything depends on it."

CHAPTER

NINE

"It's November."

Atticus smirked. "Yes, I'm aware. You bought me the calendar with the rabbits on it, remember?"

"They're kittens." Maggie tossed her suitcase down on the hotel bed with a smirk. "But they're throwing the October Revolution Parade tomorrow."

"Right."

Maggie planted her fists on her hips. "In *November*."

Atticus chuckled. "When the October Revolution happened Russia still operated under the Eastern Orthodox calendar, so it was November everywhere else. When the Soviets took control they adopted the Western calendar."

"Oh, that makes sense, I guess, in a Russian kind of way."

On their way to the National Hotel in central Moscow, Atticus and Maggie had passed blocked-off streets, scaffolding for parade seating and fresh-faced soldiers on every corner. There was a sense of anticipation in the air. The entire Soviet Union, indeed the world, would be watching the pomp and circumstance of the parade. It was made all the more significant by the fact that it was the first appearance by the newly crowned leader, Leonid Brezhnev. Just how long he held the position would be up to Atticus and Maggie.

Getting into Moscow had been easier than Atticus had imagined. Before he arrived in the sixties he'd assumed travel between the USSR and the West was reserved for diplomats and spies. It turns out it was somewhat looser than that. The USSR even had an official state travel agency, Intourist, which translated to "foreign tourist". Of course, the KGB would keep close tabs on foreign visitors, and it was almost guaranteed that one's guide would be an employee of the KGB. The guide assigned to Maggie and Atticus certainly was. The fact that he also worked for the CIA meant he wouldn't get in the way of their operation.

On arrival in Moscow they were introduced to Boris, their KGB/CIA "tour guide". Atticus wondered how he kept track of all his identities. Over the space of two hours Maggie and Atticus modelled for photos in different outfits around central Moscow. In a week's time when Boris reported back, he'd present the photos to his superiors as proof the two were nothing more than the businesspeople their visas professed them to be. After their photo shoot, Boris went off to sit in a hotel for a week to smoke, read books and order room service. Atticus thought Boris had the better part of the deal.

Maggie and Atticus were posing as representatives of the Milk Marketing Board, and had a suitcase of material to prove it. Atticus had read a few brochures before becoming deathly bored and almost blacking out. He hoped no officials wanted to grill him on milk yields and mid-lactation bodyweights to evaluate cow production efficiency on commercial dairy farms. The fact that he knew even that much gave him a headache.

"How are you going with," Maggie waved her hand around, "all this? You seem to always be running, trying to fix everything. I just want to make sure you're okay."

Atticus placed his hand gently on the side of her face. "That's sweet. *You're* sweet. I'm not going to lie, it's... a lot. When I first arrived in this time I was hoping just to witness history, not make it. Be an innocent bystander, you know?" He let go of her face and sighed. "Okay fine, if I'm honest, I thought I might poke history once in a while. Go to Queen's first gig and maybe tell Freddie Mercury that he should stick with it, that kind of thing. Because from then on I could have this self-satisfied grin every time Queen came on the radio, knowing that I in some small way made them what they were. But that's as far as I ever wanted to get. Quiet, smug, delusional self-satisfaction. Not be the cause of world-ending hysteria, which is kind of the opposite of the vibe I was aiming for. Subtle, not obvious."

Amused, Maggie shook her head. "I don't think anyone's referred to Armageddon as 'obvious' before."

"You know what I mean."

She grinned. "The scary thing is, I actually do."

Atticus opened the wardrobe and took out two suitcases that had been stashed there by the MI6 Moscow Station hours before their arrival. Inside was everything they'd need for their mission. It was easier than going through customs and having to explain why you had pistols, comms gear, sniper rifles, liquid explosives and grappling hooks in your luggage. No matter what era you were in, customs agents never had a sense of humour.

"Where to first? I'm thinking we reconnoitre the prestige parts of the parade route, scout for where Communist officials will be ferried in and out."

As she said this, Maggie extracted a Baretta, loaded it and flicked on the safety. She did the same with Atticus's Colt 1911 and handed it to him, all without batting an eyelid, as casual as if she were buttering toast.

Atticus couldn't help but beam. "That's one of the sexiest things you've ever done."

Placing a hand on her hip, Maggie cocked an eyebrow. "One of?"

Giving his best roguish smile, Atticus said, "The list is as extensive as it is creative."

"Damn fucking right." Maggie gave him a wink. "Shall we get to it?"

"Sure, but let's reconnoitre first."

"Now who's being sexy?" She crinkled her nose. "I think I like going on missions with just the two us. Feels far less restrained."

"We can use restraints if you want." Atticus placed the suitcases in the wardrobe. "If you ask nicely."

Maggie gave him a low purr as they headed out the door, and for a moment it was almost as if the fate of the world didn't rest on their shoulders.

HAVING NEVER ATTENDED an October Revolution parade before, Atticus was unsure if the over-the-top preparations were because tomorrow's event was the first public appearance of the newly anointed leader, or if they were the norm. He assumed if the Russian people didn't have Eurovision to look forward to, they may as well enjoy a wildly elaborate parade of military might.

The snow-speckled streets were awash with red flags adorned with hammers and sickles. Banners of Lenin and Marx were everywhere. Stalin, not so much. The USSR seemed eager to wash that period from their collective memory. But by far the greatest volume of posters and banners were reserved for Brezhnev.

To Atticus, Brezhnev appeared to be the quintessential Soviet leader. Meaty jowls, stern countenance and eyebrows you could play hide and seek in. He was the personification of a Communist autocrat. If the sheer volume of posters with his grave mug were any indication, State was going all out to welcome the new leader.

The former leader, Khrushchev, had grown unpopular with his own party following a trip to the US where he was hailed by the West but castigated by his own people. Add to that the worsening relations with Communist China and his time was over. A virtual coup led by Brezhnev and Shelepin forced him into "voluntary" retirement. Atticus assumed Oliver's plan must have been for Brezhnev to do the heavy lifting to oust Khrushchev, then do the same to him with Shelepin when the time was right—which must have been soon. Removing a new and unproven leader was far easier than ousting an established one. Oliver was many things, but he certainly wasn't stupid.

Atticus assumed Brezhnev had no idea there was a plot to oust him in a matter of months. And he was equally certain that even those who were behind it, Oliver included, failed to realise their machinations could propel the world into nuclear Armageddon.

At least, until that moment that's what Atticus assumed.

As they walked across the Bolshoy Moskvoretsky Bridge Atticus gulped. Until just now, he hadn't contemplated that the global catastrophe the Older Atticus had relayed might have been a deliberate act. He really hoped Oliver wasn't hell-bent on a global suicide mission. That would certainly complicate matters.

The weather was freezing. November in Russia was bleak; even Hitler found that out. Both Maggie and Atticus wore heavy coats and fur hats. It helped them blend in.

This part of Moscow was recognisable to Atticus, but not from this period. He'd been to Moscow on numerous occasions and lost count of how many times he'd walked the same bridge. The Kremlin appeared as he remembered it, and the chilly, inhospitable weather was just as familiar, but there were certainly differences, too. For one, the people were more dour and they weren't preoccupied with mobile phones. In Atticus's time, the cars in this part of the city were flashy and ostentatious, driven by equally osten-tatious oligarchs who'd rushed in to fill the Soviet void once the wall crumbled. The cars putting past now were quaintly ancient and all very similar. Atticus recalled that the corner of Balchug Street, which now hosted a flower stand, would eventually become a Starbucks.

Roadblocks had been set up at the end of the bridge closest to the Kremlin. Crisp-suited soldiers stood rigidly, guns at the ready, as alert as the USSR itself. The logistics in staging this celebration must have been monumental. Hundreds of thousands of troops, all the party officials in attendance plus the huge crowds who turned up to see the might of the Union of Soviet Socialist Republics. They all had to be fed and housed somewhere.

Even from the distance of decades into the future, where Atticus knew all this bombastic posturing would be for nought, he couldn't help getting caught up in the cere-mony of it. After all, wasn't that the point? Making the people believe in something bigger than themselves, convincing them they were on the mighty side of right? If he wasn't focused on the mission, Atticus would have revelled in seeing this piece of history unfold. Nobody did pomp like the Soviets.

"You look a million miles away."

Maggie's gleaming grin brought him back to the here and now.

"Just a few decades." He pointed towards the end of the bridge. "It seems like they'll be herding the official cars that way. Probably a good place to start."

The plan, although Atticus thought it generous to label it as such, was to follow Oliver from the parade to his place of residence, and hopefully convince him to correct the error of his ways. If that failed, they would be forced to seek a more permanent solution.

They assumed he would be attending the celebration. Oliver was drawn to power, and there was no greater show of strength on the globe than a Soviet parade. Atticus was sure he would be there. He had to be.

At the end of the Bolshoy Moskvoretsky Bridge a checkpoint had been set up, and there was a space for what appeared to be a car park. Logic told Atticus that official cars would be sent through the checkpoint, officials unloaded and then the shiny government cars would wait there to ferry them back to their luxurious homes.

The makeshift checkpoint comprised of a tall thin military tent and two equally tall and thin soldiers with clipboards. Even though the parade was twenty-four hours away, the two pimply teenagers manning the checkpoint stood rigidly upright, as if ready to receive Lenin himself.

Pretending to take in the flowing Moskva River, Atticus leant over the railing casually.

"I can cause a distraction, get the guards away from the checkpoint to give you enough time to take photos of their paperwork. They might have an itinerary or a list of approved officials."

Maggie screwed her mouth to one side. "I have a better idea."

She explained her plan. As far as Atticus was concerned, it wasn't better. In fact, he downright loathed it.

Try as he might, he couldn't dispute the logic of it, however. And he really tried. But whatever his personal feelings, the mission came first. After a good five minutes of trying to poke holes in her suggestion, he gave up and reluctantly gave Maggie a nod of approval. He just couldn't bring himself to verbalise it.

She gave him a wink, undid the top few buttons of her coat and sashayed towards the checkpoint. Sashayed was an accurate description. As Maggie moved towards the two soldiers she swung her hips like a burlesque dancer. Normally Atticus thoroughly enjoyed watching Maggie do that. Now, not so much.

Her plan was to flirt with the soldiers and find out as much as she could. Her Russian was flawless, she even had a Moscow accent. Atticus had no doubt she was up for the task, but still, he was uncomfortable with the thought of it.

It was just how espionage worked. In Atticus's time, a lot of the work involved obtaining data and sifting through the mountains of servers to find the golden nugget of evidence. Yes, there was always a place for field agents, but on the whole, a lot of modern espionage took place in climate-controlled rooms continents away from the threat.

Seduction had always been an established weapon of war. Empires had fallen because of it. There was a reason the term "honey trap" was so well known; because it worked. Spies had used their feminine charms on stupid men for as long as espionage had existed. Maggie had received training on that very subject. It didn't mean Atticus had to like it.

He watched her approach the two soldiers and they automatically relaxed their shoulders and began chatting with her. Knowing he should be watching with an air of detachment, Atticus fought an internal battle of logic and emotion. Perhaps he wasn't as well adjusted about being on missions with Maggie as he thought. He reminded himself it was the job, that Maggie was just playing a part.

He was only partially successful.

To distract himself, he whistled the opening to the 1990 power ballad "Wind of Change" by metal hair band the Scorpions. He then recalled the lyrics, which were oddly prophetic.

"Follow the Moskva. Down to Gorky Park. Listening to the wind of change."

There was a rumour that the song wasn't actually written by the Scorpions but was in fact penned by the CIA to usher in the end to communism. It was a theory so wild it was probably true. After all, Voice of America was broadcast to Warsaw Pact countries for decades, and artists like Louis Armstrong, Nina Simone and Bruce Springsteen had toured on CIA-sponsored tours. The USSR fell apart a year after the song was released, so who was Atticus to argue?

As casually as he could, Atticus glanced towards the checkpoint. The stern and official young soldiers now appeared to be nothing of the sort. Their posture had transformed from rigid planks of wood to malleable reeds gravitating towards Maggie's beaming smile and gyrating shoulders.

Focusing on the churning waters of the Moskva, Atticus

did his best to act casual for all sorts of reasons. It was a glacial ten minutes before Maggie returned.

She walked past him and mumbled without turning, "Am I good or what?"

They rendezvoused over the bridge and away from her new fanbase.

Beaming, Maggie took a little bow when Atticus arrived. "Did you see me decking those tickets? What a flashkick!" She did a little spin before composing herself. "Okay, so here's the skinny. Parade starts at eleven, we knew that. As suspected, all the bigwigs will be moseying through that gate. Brezhnev not included. Apparently he and the big honcho cronies use a special executive tunnel, like, of course they fucking do because everyone is equal but some are more equal than others. But here's the best bit: my new mates Nikolay and Dmitriy said their entrance is designated as элита стоянка . As in, 'elite parking'." Sarcasm dripped from her words. "Because nothing says absence of the social classes like your own executive parking lot. Anyway, Oliver's not on that list, buuuuut, he's on the элита ступня list. Meaning 'foot elite', which translates to the red *red* carpet, the foot entrance for party hacks who are the chosen few who don't have a fancy State car. That means we should be able to follow him on foot when he leaves. Nikolay reckons that will be around four o'clock."

"You got all that in the space of a few minutes?"

There was no hiding her glee. "I don't think I'm terrible at this field work stuff."

"You're really not." Atticus watched a passing group of soldiers marching in precise formation. "You flirt well."

"I…" Maggie tilted her head. "I don't know how to take that."

"To be honest, I didn't know how to give it."

The delight on her face washed away instantly. "We're okay, aren't we?"

Atticus turned to her and took her hand. "Of course. I'm being a douchebag."

"A... what?"

Atticus chuckled. "An idiot. A fool. You did an amazing job extracting vital information and I sat there like a dickhead brooding because my girlfriend was flirting with some dude."

"I wasn't—"

"Of course you weren't. You were doing your job, which is far more than I was doing. Sorry, temporary jealousy for absolutely unfounded and ridiculous reasons. You did great work. You saved us valuable time and were supremely efficient at it. I am filled with nothing but admiration."

Maggie gave him an impish wrinkle of her nose. "You're kind of cute when you're jealous."

Atticus grimaced. "It's hardly a redeeming trait. Sorry, it won't happen again."

"Men... men don't do a lot of apologising in the sixties. Do they do that more in your time?"

"Not as much as they should." Atticus put his hand on her shoulder. "You did great. Thank you."

"He looks happy, doesn't he?"

"Like the cat who's just fucked the canary," Maggie replied.

Atticus frowned. "Pretty sure that's not how the saying goes."

Oliver Preston, former MI6 Business Support Officer,

double agent, newly anointed USSR citizen and senior member of the KGB, stood just seven people away from the new General Secretary of the Soviet Union. It was quite the ascension. To go from being a supposed nobody at MI6 to seven steps away from the leader of the communist world was an act of astounding ladder-climbing. If Atticus ever needed a reminder—he didn't—to never underestimate Oliver, this was it.

Oliver stood towards the back, just behind Shelepin. The architect behind the architect.

Atticus and Maggie watched the party elite acknowledge the passing parade from their position in the crowd in Red Square. And what a parade. The endless flow of military might was as impressive as it was terrifying. The crown jewel was the A-350, the Soviet Union's first anti-ballistic missile. Sixty feet long, it would soon scare the hell out of every Western intelligence agency.

Maggie and Atticus couldn't get any closer, so they used binoculars to see the great and powerful men on the balcony of authority. The average citizen would never be allowed to come so close to their leaders, and were resigned to cheering them on from afar.

It was the first time Atticus had seen Oliver since their last confrontation in London. He'd managed to slip through their fingers then; they couldn't afford to let that happen again. Atticus gripped the binoculars so tight it felt like they were about to shatter.

The long-winded and bombastic October Revolution Parade went on forever. Initially an enjoyable throwback to an era before Atticus's time, the endless procession of marching soldiers, flag-waving children, tanks and nuclear missiles soon grew tedious. After the third hour it all blurred into one and Atticus feared he'd fall into a communist coma.

Fortunately, Brezhnev seemed to be in a similar mindset. Maggie elbowed Atticus, drawing his attention to the grand dais. With a yawn, Brezhnev waved to the crowd and left, and was soon followed by all his cronies, Oliver included. The parade marched on, but without its leader and key officials. Even those in charge had a limit to their staunch patriotic jingoism.

Atticus caught Maggie's eye. "We're on."

They moved into position near the end of the bridge, doing their best to be casual comrades for the next twenty minutes. They scrutinised the face of every person leaving via the official party exit. Their casualness evaporated the instant they saw him.

Hunched over, the innocuous little bespectacled man braced himself against the cold and drudged down the road to the left of their position. They followed, Maggie ahead, her features concealed beneath her fur hat, and Atticus fifty yards behind her.

Not for the first time, Atticus longed for a few drones, an interconnected team in a myriad of vehicles coupled with satellite tracking and CCTV networks. Instead, he had to settle for two humans on foot. It wasn't exactly the gold standard surveillance he was used to, but it would have to do.

They'd chosen clothing that blended in with the other Muscovites. Their coats were reversable, as were their hats. At varying times during their pursuit they'd each joined groups walking the same way. Once Oliver turned a corner they would reverse their hat or coat and walk alone. Another corner, another jacket reversal and they walked arm in arm among a group walking the same way. After that they'd walked separately, keeping him in their sights the whole way.

The goal of surveillance is to always be "quiet"; that is, no unnecessary movement or changes in direction. The idea was always to be as invisible as possible.

It occurred to Atticus that Oliver must have felt supremely comfortable, as it appeared he'd deployed no counter-surveillance strategies at all. No abrupt stops. He never once suddenly stopped to reverse his course, nor did he slow to watch reflections in windows or use any other techniques he was well versed in. Oliver seemed to believe he was untouchable here, buried deep in the bosom of the Soviet Union.

Even without high-tech tools at their disposal, Maggie and Atticus worked effortlessly, each anticipating the other's moves, always working in tandem to keep Oliver within sight. It should have been no surprise to Atticus that he and Maggie instinctively worked so well as a team. It was like they'd been doing it for years.

After half an hour, Atticus was in the lead when Oliver slowed in front of a luxurious apartment block on a leafy street and extracted a set of keys from his pocket. The rows of matching apartment buildings were all the same height, making it feel more like Paris than Moscow.

If he didn't know better, Atticus would have said this was the wealthy part of town. Of course, a communist regime would never allow such disparity. Atticus almost laughed out loud. Oliver was moving up in the world. As soon as his prey slipped through the front door, Atticus sprinted towards the apartment block.

There were eight mailboxes were situated beside the ornate front door, which was locked. Using his trusty lock-picks, Atticus opened the door and carefully scanned the opulent foyer to ensure there was no one present. The marble floors were immaculate and shiny. There was no elevator, so the grand open stairway was the only way to the upper floors. He could still hear footsteps, meaning Oliver's apartment was likely to be on one of the top floors.

Atticus stepped into the entrance tentatively. Pistol in pocket, he knocked on the door of apartment one. A squat, heavy-set woman opened the door.

In an angry impatient tone, she asked in Russian, "What?"

"Good afternoon, comrade." He flashed a smile at the same time as he flashed a KGB ident card. The woman's eyes went wide in fear. "The new tenant, the short man with glasses, what apartment number is he?"

"Nnnnine," the woman spluttered.

Atticus tilted his head in thanks and the woman retreated into her apartment in a panic. He opened the front door to the apartment block and caught Maggie's attention across the street. He held up nine fingers, pointed to his watch, held up three fingers, then made a zero. Maggie gave a thumbs up. He closed the front door silently.

Moving stealthily to the fourth landing, Atticus cautiously made his way to the ninth apartment and gave a friendly knock.

The door was wrenched open. "Da?"

"Hello Oliver." Atticus held the pistol to his forehead. "Been a while."

TEN

"You cry out, you're dead." Atticus pushed the gun barrel into Oliver's forehead for effect. "You make a run for it, you're dead. You try to signal anyone, you're dead."

With his free hand, Atticus shoved Oliver back into the apartment. Before forcing him into an armchair, he gave the traitor a pat down, and checked the chair for concealed weapons for good measure. Anyone who underestimated Oliver didn't last long.

Oliver sat heavily. "I imagine the list of things that will result in my death is quite extensive." He blew out a lungful of air. "Is there a list of things that will keep me alive, or is that as short as your attention span?"

"I'm here to talk, Oliver."

"The gun in your hand says otherwise."

"Would you have let me in without it?"

"Who can say? A present never goes astray."

Atticus rocked his head from side to side, then extracted a bottle of Laphroaig from his pocket.

"A peace offering. Thought you might appreciate a gift from home."

Instead of showing appreciation, Oliver's face hardened. "This is my home now."

Acknowledging the statement with a frown, Atticus replied, "Fine. Call it a house-warming gift, then."

Atticus returned to the entrance, placed the bottle on the hall table near the front door and took in the apartment. It was modern, especially by 1964 Soviet standards. Light-filled and spacious, it was filled with luxurious furniture. It was more akin to New York of the time than a staid communist bloc apartment.

Outside, it was getting dark; with the lights on, their meeting would be observable from other apartments. Atticus scrutinised the walls.

"The light switch is to your left."

Flicking the lights off, Atticus said, "Thanks." Glancing around him again, he added, "Nice digs."

"The Soviet Union values its key minds." Even from his position of subjugation, Oliver glared at Atticus with disdain. "They do not treat them as inferior, nor punish them with menial drudgery, working for the weak and brainless."

"I missed you too."

"I doubt that."

Atticus sighed. He had hoped things wouldn't become acrimonious so quickly. "I'm not here to argue ideology, I'm just here to talk."

Oliver folded his arms. "Then talk."

"You're making a mistake backing Shelepin."

That got his attention. While he did his best to remain neutral, several facial tics gave him away.

"Who?"

"You're going with who? Really?" Atticus rolled his eyes. "You would have been better off with I don't know what you're talking about. Or your mum. Or anything really. Especially given that you were standing next to the guy an hour ago. So, let's start again, shall we? Backing Shelepin will not end well, for you or anyone else."

Oliver pushed back his glasses and narrowed his eyes. "You killed everything I loved."

Atticus leaned against the kitchen table, pistol still trained on Oliver. "In my defence, he tried to kill me first. Oh, and let's not forget that he bombed MI6, killing twenty-seven. Some of whom were people you worked with for years, Oliver."

He was surprised it had taken this long for the subject of Mikhail to come up. Atticus wasn't about to point out that he hadn't been the one to pull the trigger. It was his father, Thomas, who had killed Mikhail. Atticus doubted Oliver would care for the semantics of the matter.

Oliver lowered his head, as he did his tone. "I'm going to repay that favour, Atticus Wolfe. *I'm* going to kill everything *you* love."

Atticus sighed. They were off topic. Then again, clearly Oliver needed to say what he had to say before they could cover the matter at hand without distraction.

"I assume it was you who destroyed Ganim's base in Siberia?" Oliver tilted his head. "There are some who would see that as an act of war."

"Me?" Atticus fluttered his eyelids, as innocent as a newborn deer. "I was in the bath at the time." He held his palms under his chin angelically. "Reading the bible. With a nun."

Groaning, Oliver rolled his eyes. "Fine. What is it you want to discuss before you kill me?"

"I'm here to save you, Oliver."

"My god, you really have found religion."

Atticus shook his head slowly. He hoped his face was as serious as his words. "You're about to make a huge mistake. I'm sure it won't feel like it at the time, but believe me, you're destined to go down in history as one of the most evil men who ever lived."

"That right?" Oliver's sarcasm conveyed his thoughts on the matter.

"You'll be mentioned in the same breath as Hitler, parking inspectors and spin class instructors."

Oliver sneered. "Thanks to you, I've studied the latter half of the twentieth century. I can't say it was pleasant reading, seeing the sad decline of such a noble and powerful union. Your book doesn't exactly paint a rosy picture for the world once the Soviet state crumbled. In fact, I would go so far as to say it became worse. A lot worse. The terrorism, the crime, the poverty." He unfolded his arms and leaned forward. "I'm going to change it. All of it. Brezhnev's not only a buffoon, he's wrong. The man's an appeaser when what we need is a lion." He waved to his bookshelves as if they held the very history itself. "He should have struck in the seventies when the imperialist United States was on its knees. They'd lost the Vietnam War and were facing a fuel crisis, skyrocketing unemployment and double-digit inflation, the collapse of the manufacturing sector, and a three hundred per cent rise in the price of basic consumer goods. They were on their knees, begging to be overthrown. And what did Brezhnev do? *Nothing.*" He spat the word. "Absolutely nothing. It should have been the era of triumph. Instead it was the era of stagnation. Those are the words your history book used. 'The era of stagnation.'" He shook his head. "The Soviet Union needs someone strong in power, who knows what it takes to shape the world. The US is weak right now and they'll only get weaker. Johnson will soon be marred by the Vietnam War. Nixon is stronger—a crook, sure, paranoid even, but more decisive, more of an alpha dog. If we want to shape the world, the time is now."

"That's why you're putting Shelepin in charge?"

Oliver frowned. "I'm more interested in how you knew what I had in mind."

"You're not denying it, then?"

"You're the one with the gun. Why bother?"

Atticus lowered the weapon, but was still ready to fire at his foe at any second. "I know a lot about what's about to transpire, Oliver."

"Your future is no more. The past you remember won't unfold. You altered all that by betraying me. It's all changed now. You couldn't possibly know anything about me or what I have planned for Shelepin."

"That's not the future I'm talking about."

Before Oliver could protest further, Atticus told him what was about to unfold. The betrayal of Brezhnev, Shelepin's ascension to power thanks to Oliver's guiding hand. Then he dropped the kicker: the uncontrolled escalation of international tensions leading to the destruction of Saigon.

That got through to Oliver. Even if he only partially believed what Atticus was telling him, nobody likes being told they're going to be the cause of millions of deaths. Little did he know, Atticus wasn't done yet.

"You would hope that would cause the world to take a step back, recognise they'd gone too far and seek a peaceful cessation of hostilities. But by then it was too late. Nobody could wind it back, and despite efforts on all sides the world continued to spiral downward into chaos and death. We fucked up, and took the world to the brink of all-out nuclear war, Oliver. Saigon was only the start; it's probably going to get worse from there, a lot worse. And by that I mean it could easily escalate to *actual* all-out nuclear war. If that happens, no one wins, not you, not me, not the West, not even the great and powerful Soviet Union. There'll be no one left alive to claim victory, Oliver."

Once again, Atticus was reminded that he didn't know the full story. He was almost certain Older Atticus had only told him part of what had happened in his time, and he highly suspected Saigon wasn't the only city bombed. The sullen expression on his older self's face whenever he spoke about the uncontrolled retaliation was enough to hint at the true horrors he'd witnessed. Atticus wished he had the full story to tell Oliver, but what he had was gruesome enough. At least, he hoped it would be.

"Even though we've been at each other's throats for a long time, I take no pleasure in informing you that it is all your fault. You did this." He shook his head. "You *will* do this, unless you stop your plans, now, today. There's still time before millions die."

Oliver didn't immediately respond. Fair enough. It wasn't every day you were told you were set to become one of the greatest mass murderers in history, that you might cause the end of the human race, or at the very least a few million lives in Southeast Asia.

Gulping, Oliver asked, "Where did you get this information?"

"From someone I trust."

"You only trust yourself."

"It's funny that you say that..." Atticus did his best to sound understanding. "Look, Oliver, you told me you want to build a more just world. Fine. We both do. We happen to differ on the dogma, sure, but ultimately we want people to be happy and safe. Dying at the base of a mushroom cloud is neither of those things." Atticus took a breath. "That's why I'm here. We both know I could just put a bullet in your head but I'm giving you a chance to set this right, to undo whatever scheme you have in place for Shelepin. If you continue on your path, no one wins. Not the East, not the West. There's no victor, only death."

Steepling his fingers before his lips, Oliver took a moment. "Why are you holding me responsible for this?"

"Because you are?"

"No, I'm not." He shook his head. "Let's pretend for one ludicrous second you're right, that you have Nostradamus's magic eight ball and can tell the future. Fine. I've had a few vodkas today, I'll go along with it for a moment. I'll even suspend all logic and pretend Shelepin somehow makes a decision that takes us to the brink of nuclear annihilation." He waved his hand. "But even if all that nonsense were true, it's not Shelepin's fault. It's not my fault." He tilted his head. "No, there is only one person who would be responsible. Only one man who is guilty of bringing the superpowers to blows." He cast an accusatory finger. "That person is you, Atticus Wolfe. You have become Death, the destroyer of worlds."

"Why do you think I'm trying to stop it?"

"Wow. Just wow." Oliver slapped his hands together. "I have to give you points for originality, I must say. You almost had me. I haven't figured out the angle yet, but damn, I have to hand it to you for originality. Nicely done."

"There's no angle, Oliver. I'm trying to right a wrong." He leaned forward. "All the wrongs."

"Sure."

"I... I'm not trying to mislead you, Oliver."

"That'd be a first." Oliver waggled a finger at him. "It's obvious you're desperately trying to stop me from having the rightful ideology to win the Cold War. I still don't really understand why. You yourself told me about the inequality in your time. The haves and the have nots. The one per cent, you called them, the super rich. Surely you can see the world would be better under Communism? It wouldn't have to be as harsh as the Russians have made it, not after we win. It would be better for all, especially you."

Atticus's eyes narrowed. "What do you mean by that?"

"You're a black man." Oliver gestured at him with his hand. "You yourself said that in your era things are difficult for black people the world over. Communism would end all that, we would all be equal."

"Hate to tell you, Oliver, but that's not the way it plays out in practicality. And I have to say, Russia in the future is no safe haven for gay people."

Oliver winced. It seemed he still wasn't comfortable with the term. Atticus assumed he'd kept that part of himself shielded from his new "friends".

"You don't know how this would play out when my approach wins."

"I hate to tell you but I do, and it's not pretty." Atticus realised he was straying from his intent. "Like I said, it would have been easier to just kill you, but I wanted to give you a chance to fix the chaos you're about to create. Believe me, you don't want what's coming. No one does."

"You said yourself you don't know what I already have in place, so I'd call it less altruism and more opportunism. Did you really expect to ensure the downfall of the Soviet Union with a five-minute chat? Do you think that little of me, old friend?" The revulsion was plain in his tone. "You killed Mikhail, you humiliated me, exposed me, tried to kill me on multiple occasions and now you come here with a ludicrous story that you have absolutely no way of knowing is true and expect me to suddenly kowtow to the great and powerful Atticus Wolfe? You really are a fool."

"I'm trying to help you, us, everyone."

Oliver shook his head. "Your ridiculous story is just that —a story. You've wasted your time coming here, you pathetic little man."

"Ganim succeeded in building a working time machine."

The statement surprised them both. It wasn't something Atticus had planned to divulge.

"He's nowhere near—"

"In a year's time he will be." Atticus cut him off and went on. "He managed to send a… message back in time to tell us how badly things get screwed up. A year from now Saigon is obliterated, the West about to retaliate. What Ganim did was the last Hail Mary of a planet on the brink of destruction. This knowledge gives us a chance to fix things. That's how I know, Oliver, because it's already happened."

It took a moment for Oliver to process this new information. In the end, he frowned. "If you're trying to appeal to my better self, you of all people should know I don't have one."

Atticus's desperate last-ditch attempt to turn the tide was failing. He'd known it would be a long shot trying to reason with Oliver. Older Atticus had argued against it; stridently so. There was still a part of Atticus who hoped a remnant of the old Oliver had survived. A man of reason, a man who would see the truth and do everything he could to stave off potential Armageddon.

Atticus realised once again how wrong he'd been. Older Atticus had been right all along.

Reluctantly, he raised the pistol. If he were honest with himself, he'd suspected this was how it would end. It was the only way to be sure. The chaos of history would end here.

With a *crack* the front door burst open and two heavy-suited men burst through the breach. In the fraction of a second as they entered, their guns searching for targets, Atticus's instincts kicked in automatically. He wondered how Oliver's protectors knew he was there. *The light switch.* It must have been a trigger, to communicate that Oliver was a hostage.

It was fortunate that Oliver wasn't the only one who was prepared for all eventualities.

In the fraction of a second it took the KGB goons to zero in on Atticus, he fired. Aiming between the two men, who contorted their bodies to target the new threat, Atticus fired at the whiskey bottle by the front door.

Except it wasn't whiskey.

The ensuing fireball engulfed the two men in a corrosive flaming ball of death. Chlorine trifluoride was a terrible way to die. As the two walking corpses tried in vain to extinguish the flames boiling their skin from their bodies, Oliver bolted for the bedroom and dove through the double doors. Atticus fired after him, hitting the door as it slammed shut.

The bullets didn't penetrate the wooden door. That's because it wasn't wooden.

A heavy *thunk* reverberated through the metal reinforced doors, as if a heavy metal crossbar had been slammed into place on the other side. Knowing it pointless, Atticus shouldered the door regardless, then staggered backwards from the painful manifestation of Newton's third law of motion. A human body was not going to defeat a heavy metal reinforced door. Bullets weren't getting through either.

As the two flaming bodies collapsed and noxious smoke engulfed the apartment, shouts emanated from the hallway, no doubt reinforcements for the corpses slumped in the burning doorway. The frame was alight, as was the nearby kitchenette, but that wouldn't hold the KGB back for long. With Oliver shut off in the bedroom, Atticus had only one option.

Kicking open the glass doors to the balcony, Atticus glanced down. The apartments below had no balconies and it was too far to jump, unless he fancied two broken legs. He gazed up to the balcony above, then the roof, and then tucked the pistol into the back of his trousers. "Fuck it."

He climbed onto the railing of Oliver's balcony, then leapt, just managing to grasp the bottom railing of the balcony above. Using every ounce of strength from his gym-deprived arms, Atticus heaved himself skyward, up and over the railing. As he tumbled onto the balcony, Atticus heard heavy footsteps burst into Oliver's apartment below.

Gawping through the window beside him, Atticus was confronted with a robust man in an army peaked cap and the jacket of an Army General. His lower half was not as militarily adorned. In fact, not only did the man not have any pants on, he wasn't wearing underwear, either. His bottom half only sported gartered socks. The pantsless General stared blankly at Atticus. He didn't make any sudden moves, just gawped, open-mouthed.

Two choices were immediately open to Atticus - either a pantsless hostage situation or a shootout on the stairwell as he fought his way down several floors. Both would have the same terminal result. He needed a third option.

Atticus leapt towards the drain pipe and climbed. Muscles screaming for respite, he clambered upward, gritting his teeth as he did. This wasn't how this was meant to end. He cursed himself for taking so long in appealing to Oliver's humanity. The man was too far gone, their rivalry too great for reason. And Oliver had obviously been expecting Atticus. Why else would he have had a huge iron door constructed in his apartment? Atticus should have executed him the second he'd arrived. Now he'd lost all chance of ending Oliver's destructive path.

Scampering over the lip of the roof, Atticus was thankful for Soviet craftmanship as the gutter held firm. He rolled onto his back and took a moment to suck in welcome cool air. Forcing himself into movement, Atticus hurried across the tiled roof in a crouch, gun at the ready. He had to be mindful of his steps lest he slip and fall five floors to his death.

But soon that was the least of his concerns.

The *crack* of the gunshot reverberated around the surrounding buildings. Unsure where it had come from, Atticus instinctively dove, landing hard on the tiles. The force of the landing involuntary propelled the gun to bounce from his hands. That wasn't the worst thing. Atticus had no grip on the roof's surface and slipped rapidly towards the edge in an uncontrolled slide. Desperately clawing at the tiles, Atticus couldn't slow his descent.

It was only when his feet hit the gutter that he came to a shuddering halt. Heaving in a relieved breath, he lifted his head to see a lone man in a suit at the apex of the roof, gun trained on Atticus.

Lifting his hands, Atticus called out, "Не листайте. Я безоружен!"

Which translated to, "Don't shoot. I'm unarmed."

The KGB agent didn't move his gun from Atticus, but he didn't fire either. That meant they wanted him alive. Not exactly as comforting as it could have been.

Slowly rising to his feet, Atticus kept his arms aloft. As he did so, he peered behind him, beyond the lip of the roof. On this side of the building there was nothing but roadway below. No balconies, no convenient awnings to break his fall. Just certain death.

He smiled at the KGB man, doing his best to appear friendly and cooperative. Unswayed by Atticus's sudden obedience, the KGB agent motioned with his gun for Atticus to come towards him, no doubt to be handed over to his comrades. Given the fact that he'd just murdered two of them in the most hideous way possible while also attempting to murder their superior, Atticus held little hope for fair and gentle treatment. All he saw in his near future was torture and death. Then probably more torture.

Gazing to his side, he regarded the gutter and gritted his teeth. *You have the absolute worst ideas, Atticus Wolfe.*

The KGB agent must have sensed a change. He yelled at Atticus to come toward him.

Atticus shook his head.

Then he dove off the roof.

ELEVEN

A s he leapt from the perfectly serviceable roof, Atticus momentarily questioned his life choices. Moscow's skyline streaked before his eyes. Seeing nothing but the brutally solid roadway below, he flew through the frigid air, his eyes turned to his one goal.

His hand darted towards the gutter as bullets flew overhead. The fingers of his left hand grasped the outer edge of the gutter and his forward motion flung his body like a pendulum upwards. He'd need the momentum.

His gun had slipped from his grasp when he was on the roof and now sat precariously upright in the gutter. As he swung upward, his right hand seized the weapon before swinging back the other way. Flinging out his legs to give him extra momentum, Atticus willed his arm muscles to give him everything they had. Swinging upward with all his might, his head just cleared the lip of the gutter to see the KGB agent, clearly startled. It was understandable. You don't usually expect a man who just leapt off the roof to reappear. Especially armed. Atticus didn't give him much time to process it. He simply fired two bullets into the centre of the man's chest.

Swinging down again, Atticus dangled from the roof, one-handed. He tossed the gun up over the roof to free his other hand. Unfortunately for him it bounced off the tiles, clanged against the gutter and fell to the road below. Atticus grunted. Better the gun than him. Exhausted, he heaved his body upward with two hands using the last remnants of strength he possessed.

It was unfortunate then, that when he poked his head up over the gutter he was confronted with the sight of the dead KGB agent sliding down the tiles, on a direct path to collide with Atticus dangling precariously. And he was coming towards him fast.

"Oh, come on!"

Gritting his teeth, Atticus gripped one screaming hand over the other, desperately trying to move along the gutter. With inches to spare, the dead KGB agent hit the gutter and, with heavy limbs flailing, silently tumbled off the roof.

The resultant splatter on the road below was an unnecessary reminder for Atticus not to fall. He inhaled unsteadily and urged any remaining vestiges of strength to propel his aching body upwards.

With throbbing muscles screeching for respite, Atticus groaned as he miraculously hauled himself up and over the roof once more. Wheezing, he lay on his back, thankful for every inhalation of sweet air into his lungs.

When he'd gathered enough energy, he said, "You have to hand it to the Soviets. They build a good gutter."

He made a mental note to send the builder a letter of thanks. Or some blue jeans. At the thought Atticus managed a chuckle to relieve some pressure. Carefully, very carefully, he crawled his way to the apex of the roof. Given how quickly the now very dead and very flat agent had managed to get himself up there, Atticus determined there must be roof access somewhere. It didn't take long before he spied the open roof hatch.

The apartments' roofs were interconnected and uninterrupted for a couple hundred feet. It was tempting to go back the way the KGB agent had come, but doing so would likely lead to more encounters with the KGB. As fun as that sounded, Atticus wanted to avoid any further gun battles if he could manage it. He just didn't have the energy. Or the firepower.

Atticus assumed his odds would be better if he could find a roof hatch further away from his starting point. Arms held wide for balance, he made his way across the roof, striving for an equilibrium between urgency and certain death.

Mumbling to himself, Atticus said, "Just one break, that's all I'm asking for."

As he neared the end of the roof, he spied other similar apartment blocks separated by the streets far below. Too far to jump to. At last, he spotted another roof access point ahead and was filled with hope.

"Стой, не двигайся!"

Sighing, Atticus stopped and pivoted slowly to see a fresh-faced KGB agent aiming a Makarov pistol at him. The guy's hand was visibly shaking. This kid must have been fresh out of the academy.

"Stay still, American!"

Even in the precarious situation he was in, Atticus grunted. "What... Why do you think I'm American?"

The KGB kid motioned the gun up and down. "You look American."

"I *look* American?" Atticus sneered. He should probably

have been concerned with other things, he knew, but he was riled. "Because I'm black. Is that it?"

The pimply KGB agent shrugged.

"Fucken racist motherfucker."

"What?"

"You heard."

"I am holding the gun!"

Atticus planted his fists on his hips. "This may come as a revelation, twat, but holding a gun doesn't make you a), less racist or b), less wrong. It just means you're the one holding the gun. You're also the one who's being racist."

"Why am I racist?"

"I... dude."

The KGB kid shrugged again. "But you look like one of those proud American black people. From the movies."

"You can be black and proud from any country, mate."

The softer stance of the KGB kid visibly hardened. "You killed many of my comrades today."

"They shot at me first."

"You burned them alive. You will come with me. There are many of my colleagues who wish to... talk with you."

"They don't actually want to talk with me, do they?"

"Possibly at first."

"And then?"

"You look like a smart man. I think you know how this will end, da?"

Atticus understood. The KGB were not renowned for hugs and pillow forts. They were the perpetrators of the most barbarous and heinous torture methods known to man. Their experts could keep someone half alive for weeks, prolonging their suffering as if this would somehow result in the subject seeing the error of their ways and divulging more truth. It was ridiculous, of course. After a day or so they'd be so out of their mind they would tell their captors anything to make the pain stop.

The KGB kid motioned for Atticus to come towards him. Atticus was disinclined to, but given his unarmed status, he didn't have much in the way of options.

The gunshot crack pierced the cold air. The KGB kid crumbled, a growing red stain at the centre of his chest.

Turning, Atticus scanned the buildings behind him. It wasn't long before he saw a woman standing on a fourth storey balcony, holding a pistol in both hands.

Maggie gave a friendly wave before tucking her gun beneath her coat. She shook her head and raised her palms inquisitively as if to say, *what the fuck are you doing?*

She had a point.

Atticus scrambled over to KGB kid and extracted the Makarov pistol from his dead-man grip, then forced open the roof hatch and made his way down to street level. It felt like hours, but it had been mere minutes since the encounter in the apartment. Nowhere near enough time for the KGB to gather enough manpower to cover all the exits.

Maggie met him on the street and the two stuck to the back streets as they made their way to anywhere else. At speed. Fire engines raced past them.

After traversing in silence for a few blocks, Atticus said, "That was one hell of a shot."

Maggie smirked. "I'm one hell of a woman."

"That you are, Maggie Dunbar, that you are."

"THIS OPERATION HASN'T GONE ENTIRELY to plan."

"Entirely, you say?" Maggie raised an eyebrow.

"Not entirely, no."

Maggie and Atticus sat in their hotel room with the curtains drawn, licking their wounds. The two sat at the end of the bed sharing a loaf of bread and a bottle of vodka; the only items resembling room service the hotel was able to provide. It was so ironically Russian they didn't mind.

"I'm sure Rathdowne would call it a cock-up."

"He calls everything a cock-up."

She wasn't wrong. Then again, she rarely was.

The two had just finished a debrief with the Moscow Station chief, who was livid that an operation had taken place on his turf without his knowledge. That was by design, of course. It would have been difficult to explain ahead of time why Oliver was so critical. Plus, the more people who knew of an operation the more likely it was to become compromised. Regardless, they'd still managed to turn it into, as Maggie so eloquently put it, a cock-up.

The fumes of the station chief's fury still lingered in the room, though the vodka was going some way towards dampening their stench. The two certainly didn't need someone else to tell them just how royally they'd screwed things up.

Not only had Atticus failed to persuade Oliver to correct his course, he'd failed to neutralise him. It was likely the man was now even more dangerous than ever.

Atticus had been surprised by just how bitter Oliver was. No, bitter was the wrong word. Vengeful was more apt. Mikhail's death had tormented his very soul. His burning rage obliterated logic. Oliver was so consumed by it, the revelation he would usher in a hot war between superpowers barely seemed to penetrate.

Atticus had grown up witnessing that kind of unquenchable rage in his father; it was ultimately why his father had spent more of his adult life in prison than out of it. The last time he was incarcerated was for beating a shopkeeper half to death for not paying protection money. While inside, he'd taken his untamed wrath out on a fellow inmate. It was unfortunate that particular inmate had a gang who ended Thomas Wolfe's life. He died alone in a shower block without a single friend in the world, his incandescent rage finally extinguished.

Atticus hoped the man he'd met in this era would grow up to be a different Thomas Wolfe. Even though he had kept his distance to avoid ruining the timeline further, Atticus hoped he'd had a positive influence on his old man. But that was a topic for another time. Atticus turned his attention back to the matter at hand.

"Putting on your psychological analyst hat, what's your recommendation on how to deal with Oliver now?"

Maggie didn't immediately respond. She steepled her fingers, mulling the topic over. Not only was she versed in psychological training, she'd worked with a team to create a profile on the man. And in addition, for years the two had been best friends. They'd shared experiences, supported one another and traversed more than a few hardships. Granted, Oliver's life had been a hall of mirrors, but no matter how good a double agent you were, some aspects of one's true personality always bled through.

After several moments of contemplation, Maggie finally said, "There's only one course of action."

"What's that?"

"The other Atticus is right. We need to kill Oliver."

TWELVE

I n life, things are often easier said than done. Take, for example, killing Oliver Preston.

By the time Atticus and Maggie had collected themselves and reported back to MI6, Oliver had left his apartment and never returned. In the days that followed, he didn't show up at the Kremlin. Nor was he spotted at or the Lubyanka Building, the KGB headquarters. Sixty MI6 agents were tasked with finding Oliver—although they didn't know why—and none found a trace.

Oliver had disappeared into the cracks of Moscow.

After a week, they all agreed the man wasn't going to be found by conventional means. Nor, it seemed, unconventional. Every asset MI6 possessed had been tasked with finding information on his whereabouts, but be it a cleaner or a senior party official with skeletons in their closet, none had a line on him.

It was frustrating to have come so close only to fail. Oliver had been literally within Atticus's grasp. Sure, he could have executed him as soon as he'd arrived, but as Rathdowne had articulated from the start, the mission was to try and reason with the man first. Whatever schemes within schemes Oliver constructed could have been undone if only he'd listened. If only he'd seen reason. Neither of those things happened.

Maggie's statement about the need to take Oliver's life had been out of character, and at first Atticus wasn't sure where it had come from. Sure, she'd pulled the trigger before, but in those instances, it had been kill or be killed. This was different. This was premeditated.

Was it because she'd finally freed herself of the shackles of the friendship the two had shared? Was it fear of Atticus's safety overriding her normal abhorrence of violence? In the end, she explained, it came down to one inevitable conclusion: they'd exhausted all other possible options. The only choice to avoid a global calamity was to end the life of the man responsible.

But in the end, it mattered little. Oliver was gone.

The recall order came later than Atticus expected, but it still came. He and Maggie were ordered to jump on the next plane out of Moscow. The mission was a bust.

They landed in London at five am, via a connecting flight in Helsinki. The two were exhausted but focused. They went straight to the Tower. There was no time to sleep.

"Do you think you got through to him?" Rathdowne poured black tea for them both.

The pair had had the exact same conversation a hundred times in the past week. The reason they'd had it so many times was because there was no definitive answer.

"I don't know for certain." Atticus sipped the bitter tea. "Optimistically, I'd like to think so, but he's still twisted from Mikhail's death. It would be difficult for anyone to believe the story I told him, let alone when hearing it from someone he's been actively trying to kill for a year." He exhaled heavily. "I just don't know. The spy in me says no."

Maggie gave him a faint smile of encouragement. Atticus wasn't sure if her washed-out expression was due to lack of sleep or the fact she didn't believe Oliver had been turned from his path of destruction. Possibly both.

Rathdowne poured himself a tea. The teapot was ornate, and out of place in his cluttered but otherwise austere office. Atticus was sure there was a story there, but he had other things on his mind. He wasn't the only one.

Since leaving Moscow, Atticus had been preparing himself for the incoming barrage of abuse from Rathdowne. It was almost more disconcerting that they hadn't received one. Rathdowne appeared distracted, uncharacteristically unfocused. It was clear something was playing on his mind, but he forged on regardless.

"The Chinese are chummy with the Soviets again now Khrushchev has sodded off. Our government's had two no-confidence motions in a week, and thanks to your photos at the October Revolution Parade, which was stupidly held in November..."

"That's what I said!" Maggie bounced in her chair.

"... all heads of the armed forces are petrified their nukes won't get through because the Reds now have anti-ballistic missiles. So, of course their response is to build more nukes." He rubbed his eyes. "And given what the other Atticus Wolfe said is in our future, I don't think more nuclear bombs is the answer to, well, anything really."

"Which is all the more reason for us get back to Moscow as soon as—"

"Speaking of which, I've been having some chats with your other self, the future one." Ignoring Atticus's interruption, Rathdowne sipped his tea. "It's hard to get the grammar right with you two. Plurals. Past tense. Future tense. I think a Cambridge professor would have a hard time with you lot."

"That's all very nice, but we can head back at—"

"He's holding back. The man's devious." Rathdowne contemplated his teacup. "And given who he is, that's saying a lot." He looked up to stare Atticus in the eye. "You've lied to me from day one. You lied to me every day after that. Sitting there in that chair, I fully expect the next thing that comes out of your mouth to be a lie."

He was right, Atticus had never told Rathdowne the complete truth and they both knew it. Even now, with Rathdowne knowing he was from the twenty-first century, that his other self had travelled back in time and just how royally they'd screwed the timeline, there were still secrets. For one, Rathdowne didn't know about Atticus and Maggie. Given the sexist times they were in, it was likely she'd be thrown out of the service before they'd even finished telling him. No, he'd never been completely truthful with Rathdowne, but the man before him was riled up beyond mere annoyance.

It seemed Atticus had an answer to what had been distracting Rathdowne since their arrival. It was him. Or rather, his other self. It seemed like Rathdowne had been stewing on this for quite some time.

Holding up a hand to stave off Atticus's inevitable counterargument to being called a liar, Rathdowne said, "But this is different. The other you," he pointed at the door, "is definitely hiding something, more than one something, I believe. I had him tell me the same story he told you lot on the plane, about how he got here. It flows along then ceases abruptly. The version he told me stopped at the same point as the one he told you, according to Ganim." He snorted. "It's bloody ridiculous, but I trust a twisted old terrorist more than I do that other Wolfe. No matter how many times in the last week I tried to get more out of him, he was as tight-lipped as the sphinx."

He stood. Atticus and Maggie exchanged glances. For one, this sudden change of subject mid-conversation was surprising. Secondly, Rathdowne had hit on their second-most talked about topic: what exactly was the other Atticus hiding?

Without further discussion, Rathdowne marched out of the office. The other two glared at the open door.

Maggie blinked several times. "Uh, do we follow him?"

"I... guess?" Atticus shook his head. "How did we go from a discussing Oliver to accusing the other me of deception?"

Maggie shook her head. "It's obviously been on his mind for ages." She popped her thumb at the door. "We better..."

"But we need to find out if we can go back to Moscow."

"We're not going to find out in an empty room, are we?"

They scurried after their boss and found him charging down the stairs. They had to run to catch up. Clearly on a mission, Rathdowne stormed down a succession of corridors until he came to a door guarded by with two Beefeaters. Without acknowledging them, Rathdowne threw open the door and barged in. Maggie gave the Beefeaters a salute and followed suit, as did Atticus.

Inside, wooden horses with suits of armour had been pushed against one wall to make room for the new centre-piece: a monstrous silver computer, replete with flashing lights and spinning tape reels. It looked like something out of *Get Smart*. It may have been state-of-the-art for the time, but Atticus couldn't help but find it quaint.

Huddled over a large wooden table covered in blue-prints, Ganim and Older Atticus raised their heads at the intrusion. The latter's beard was coming along nicely. On seeing Rathdowne's obvious ire, the two exchanged curious glances.

Older Atticus turned to his counterpart. "Survived Moscow, then?"

"Barely."

Maggie waved to Ganim. "Hi Omar."

"Lady Maggie," Ganim tilted his head in greeting, "always a pleasure."

"Can I help you, Rathdowne?"

Older Atticus's head pivoted between Younger Atticus and Rathdowne. It was virtually accusatory, as if he was silently asking what Atticus had put his boss up to.

"As a matter of fact, yes." Rathdowne planted his fists on his hips. "You can provide me with answers."

"Absolutely." Older Atticus slapped his hands together. "Okay, so the shortest recorded war in history is the Anglo-Zanzibar War, which lasted a grand total of thirty-eight minutes. Art used to be a competitive sport at the Olympics. A snail can sleep for three years."

"That's not what I meant and you know it!"

"Rabbits can't vomit?" Older Atticus suggested.

"They can't?" Maggie asked.

"Maggie," Younger Atticus said quietly, "that's not helping." He smiled. "And no, they can't."

"Look," Rathdowne's legendary tinge of red engulfed his face, "I've had enough of your evasion. I've been brooding on this for some time—"

"So it would seem."

"—and I want to know," Rathdowne motioned to all in

the room, "we all want to know what happened to you. What happened in your past, our potential future."

"I've already told you—"

"No," Rathdowne stepped forward, "you haven't. You skipped quite a bit. You said Shelepin took control, Saigon was bombed, then there were escalating tensions, then— boom—you turned up in his flat. Where's the rest of it? It's like telling the story of a marriage and going from the lovely reception where everyone had a grand time, then they got old and died. You skipped all the juicy bits."

Younger Atticus noted that when Rathdowne mentioned marriage, Older Atticus flinched.

"You're going to tell us everything," Rathdowne crossed his arms, "and you're going to tell us now."

"I can't—"

"You can and you will." Rathdowne's barely controlled anger resonated from every part of him. "If you don't, your status as a bonus MI6 employee shall be revoked faster than you can say there's too many Atticus Wolfes here already. Tell us the truth or walk out that door this very minute. The choice is yours."

Older Atticus's shoulders slunk. It took less than a minute for the rest of the group to position chairs in a semi-circle before him. Sipping on a glass of water, he seemed to be gathering his thoughts, deciding where to begin.

"Before the end, Oliver came for me."

"Here, in London?"

Older Atticus let out a slow sigh. "The man was utterly unhinged. His grand plans in tatters, he went stark raving mad. He threatened my family in Brixton. He threatened to murder everyone I loved."

"He made a similar threat to me in Moscow," Younger Atticus said.

Older Atticus nodded in acknowledgement. "You should never dismiss any threat Oliver makes."

Younger Atticus gulped. "Why do you say that?"

"Because he did it. He killed everyone I ever loved." He turned to Maggie. "Everyone."

THIRTEEN

TWELVE MONTHS IN THE FUTURE

The world went to hell.

Two days after the USSR crossed the border into Norway, every NATO country declared war. Europe was awash with refugees, troop movements and, above all else, chaos.

It had been four and a half months since Shelepin stoked the hellfire of Vietnam by actively involving the Soviets; two months since Saigon had been obliterated in an incandescent flash.

For a brief shining moment following that catastrophic event it seemed like the superpowers had retreated from the brink of mutually assured destruction. But it was all a ruse. They just needed time to prepare for battle.

After the insane carnage of two brutal world wars, people naively believed their leaders had grown out of armed conflict. They were wrong. The world careered towards the biggest conflict in history and no one could see a way to prevent it. Diplomats from all over the world had been recalled, a clear indication that diplomacy had failed. Only skeleton staff remained, to either protect their secrets or burn them.

Every country in the world called up their reserves. Most reintroduced the draft. Civilian manufacturing plants were transformed into production lines of war as everyone on the planet readied themselves for combat, the situation a powder keg waiting to ignite. Humanity waited for the inevitable spark.

But not everything was terrible. Atticus bought a ring.

When he'd entered the quaint old jeweller's he'd expected the elderly proprietor would think him mad to be worrying about an engagement ring with the world falling apart. It turned out that wasn't the case.

"No, son. This has been my busiest month ever. I think it's because no one wants to be alone when the end comes."

They'd spent an hour perusing styles and settings. Atticus finally settled for a French-set engagement ring. It had been laughably cheap compared to twenty-first century prices, but still took a sizable chunk of his savings, a couple of months' wages. The jeweller, like almost all businesses in recent weeks, only accepted cash. Credit was luxury none could afford any longer.

Ring safely tucked in his jacket pocket, Atticus headed to Ganim's laboratory in a warehouse in Greenwich.

For months Ganim and his ever-expanding team had worked tirelessly on their "supercomputer". As far as the top brass were concerned, the team soaking up millions of pounds and stealing the greatest scientific minds of the nation were building a machine to track incoming intercontinental ballistic missiles. Only a few select individuals knew they were doing nothing of the sort.

Ganim looked like a man who hadn't slept in months. Countless nights of having the fate of the world resting on his shoulders had worn the man down, not helped by his advanced years. Regardless, for the first time in a long time, he seemed genuinely happy.

As Atticus made his way across the giant warehouse full of overlapping overhead wires, huge banks of churning computers and caravans for those too exhausted to go home, he could see glee on Ganim's face. He took Atticus by the arm and led him away from the white-coated technicians, out of earshot.

"We've done it, old friend. We've fucking well done it."

"What?" Atticus was surprised, but impressed. "You said you were at least weeks away."

"We cracked the imaginary time calculations far more quickly than I'd have thought possible." Seeing the blank expression on Atticus's face, Ganim went on. "It's a mathematical representation of time incorporating special relativity and quantum mechanics. It connects quantum mechanics with statistical mechanics and certain cosmological theories. Imaginary time, mathematically, is real time which has undergone a Wick rotation so its coordinates are multiplied by the imaginary units."

Atticus was quiet for a moment. "I'm just going to go ahead and take that as a good thing."

"A very good thing."

"This calls for a celebration."

"Way ahead of you."

Ganim led Atticus to his caravan, where a bottle of champagne nestled in a bucket of ice.

"Will the," Atticus waved his hand around, "gobbledy-gook you just said work in the backup location?"

As much as Ganim, Maggie and Atticus trusted the scientists they worked with, they knew theirs was a mission others wouldn't understand. Nor could they rely on them to not abuse the power if they discovered its true purpose. That was why the mobile phone, keypad and another computer were held elsewhere, just in case.

Ganim nodded. "It will." He unwrapped the cork. "I was expecting your better half as well. Is she not coming?"

"She's going to meet us here. She had an errand to run first."

"Oh well." Ganim popped the cork. "Time waits for no man, or woman for that matter."

"You should know."

The two men shared a laugh. In the last few months they'd grown close. Regardless of their pasts, working side by side the two twenty-first century men had formed a bond. Whether due to their shared history—well, future— or working together under difficult circumstances, they had become genuine friends.

Pouring the champagne into paper cups, Ganim said, "You've been away the last few days. I assume it has something to do with our friend overseas?"

Atticus closed the caravan door. "Not him, his power mad friend. Whitehall... ordered a plan to take out the General Secretary of the USSR. I've been coordinating MI6's part in the operation."

Ganim was aghast. Rightfully so.

Holding up a hand, Atticus went on. "I've been the one in the room arguing restraint. Killing a head of state is no way to deescalate a situation. I think my voice has been heard. I don't think even the government is crazy enough to try and kill Shelepin."

"Need I remind you, we live in crazy times."

The mission to assassinate Shelepin involved elite members of MI6 and SAS. It was a last-ditch attempt to wind back the madness that had been escalating since Shelepin came to power. Under Atticus's tactical guidance they'd put in enough red tape approvals that it would be impossible for the men on the ground to pull the trigger unless it was absolutely the last choice left on the table. Even if they had to act, Atticus had created a scenario that would make it seem like senior members of the Communist Party had orchestrated the hit. He hoped they'd never need it.

The team had been in-country for five days. They were actively monitoring Shelepin's movements, but that was the extent of it. Now everything was in place, Atticus could step back slightly. His trip to the jeweller's had been the first time Atticus had left work in weeks. It was enough to remind him of a time when the fate of the world wasn't continually on his mind.

There was a knock at the caravan door. Ganim raised an eyebrow. "Yes?"

The door creaked open. It was Ganim's assistant, Whelan. He bowed his head meekly and said, "There's a telephone call for Mr Wolfe."

Atticus smiled. While he enjoyed getting phone calls from Maggie, he did miss the simplicity of text messages. Finding the person at the right address at the right time was tedious and inefficient.

Leaving his champagne behind, Atticus made his way across the vast warehouse to the far brick wall that housed a bank of telephones. Whelan pointed at the second handset, which was laying on its side, and left Atticus to it.

"Hello beautiful."

"Hello darling." The deep male voice on the other end of the line certainly wasn't the dulcet tone Atticus had anticipated.

"Rathdowne?"

"You obviously weren't expecting my call." There was a pause. "I assume."

It was the closest Rathdowne ever got to a joke.

"Sorry sir. I was expecting someone else… What's up?"

"They implemented it." Rathdowne's tenor was almost a growl. "Four hours ago. We just got word."

"Implemented what?"

"The thing they were sent to do."

Even though this was supposedly a secure line, the two men weren't taking chances. They spoke in half sentences.

"But the approval protocols…"

"Were completely ignored, as it turns out." Rathdowne's tone was even gruffer than usual. He didn't approve of this any more than Atticus did. "Strategic imperative, they said. Target was on the move."

Atticus held his breath. "And?"

"They bloody well did it."

Atticus didn't know if he should be relieved or terrified. On one hand, they'd taken out the one man who had escalated an unprecedented war stance, but on the other, the UK had just assassinated a foreign head of state. That was an act of war in anyone's books. It was hard to be pleased about that sort of thing.

"Did they deploy the decoy scenario?"

Atticus anxiously awaited the response. The plan to

frame various members of the Communist Politburo was their only hope of avoiding all-out war.

"Apparently they did. Like I said, details are sketchy at this stage."

"And the team?" Atticus had worked directly with most of them over the last few weeks.

"Two unaccounted for. Initial report indicated full success, but..."

"The missing men have you worried?"

"Correct."

"I'll be right there."

Atticus hung up without another word. This was a screw-up on a monumental scale. The team had acted without explicit authorisation; the exact thing Atticus had been trying to avoid. Tensions were high, the need to act was strong across the board, but this was recklessness on an unprecedented scale. The irresponsibility would have consequences, Atticus knew. He dreaded what they might be.

He made his way back to the caravan. Seeing Atticus's face, Ganim reeled.

"What's happened?"

Pursing his lips, Atticus said, "That thing I'd been actively trying to prevent has happened. I need to get back to the office." He motioned to the champagne. "Sorry to cut this short."

Ganim shook his head. "Don't be ridiculous. You go. If we can stop this in the here and now without having to use," he motioned outside the caravan, "all the better. This was always a backup."

Atticus didn't share the man's optimism. If all the pieces didn't fall into perfect alignment, the ramifications would be bad.

Atticus grinned. "A backup you just got working."

Picking up the paper cup, Ganim raised the drink to himself. "I fucking well did at that. We're going to be ready to live test in a week or so, but let's hope it doesn't come to that."

"I like your confidence."

There was another knock, then Whelan stuck his head through the door again.

"Mr Wolfe, you have another call."

"Jesus. Tell him I'm on my way."

"No, it's Miss Dunbar. She sounded rather... I think you should take it, sir."

He and Ganim exchanged glances, then Atticus raced to the bank of telephones.

"Maggie, what is—"

"Oh, Atticus, I'm so sorry. I'm so sorry." There was palpable distress in her voice.

"What is it?"

"You need to come here. Now."

"Where are you? Rathdowne's asked me into the office. Is this about the—"

"Sod Rathdowne. Whatever that is, it doesn't matter." Her voice cracked, and she finally broke down. "You need to get here now."

"Where are you, Maggie?"

"Brixton."

THE SCENE WAS PURE ANARCHY. Police cars, ambulances and fire trucks blocked the street. Wooden barricades cut off both ends of the road, as did swathes of police. The constabulary were doing their best to keep the massive crowd behind their barriers. The throng was a mixture of curious onlookers and those trying desperately to get past, calling the names of loved ones. Pure bedlam.

It was impossible to tell what had happened further down the usually busy main street, as it was bereft of anyone who wasn't wearing a uniform. Police cars and ambulances blocked any view of the scene. Atticus had asked a few rubberneckers what had transpired, but the answer was a series of unknowing grunts.

Making his way to the front of the crowd, Atticus waved over a young constable. "Wolfe, MI6. Can I get through?"

"MI6?" The white police officer regarded Atticus with a sneer. "Yeah, and I'm a monkey's uncle."

The constable lingered on the word *monkey*. Atticus clenched his fists. As he instinctively drew back his right fist, he heard a call behind the officer.

"Atticus!"

Maggie tugged the sleeve of a police inspector standing next to her. She pointed in Atticus's direction, and the inspector quickly ushered him through the police cordon. He glared at the sneering constable as he passed, daring him to make another crack, but he wisely remained silent.

The instant Atticus was within range, Maggie launched herself into his arms with a flurry of sobs and overlapping words. It was hard to determine anything she was saying. A few key words tumbled out. Restaurant. Staff. Customers. There was one word that made him stop breathing: *family*.

"What do you mean, Maggie? You're not making sense. What's happened?"

"The restaurant," she managed to get out. "In the restaurant, they're... they're..."

The older inspector spoke up. "It's a professional hit as far as we can ascertain." His detached tone was that of one professional speaking to another. "The Yard doesn't think it's gang related. For once I agree. Hunted Nazis in France, I did. I can tell you this is not the work of amateurs. The way they took out the targets—"

Atticus was no longer listening. He was running.

Weaving past flat-footed police and ambulance crews, he made his way to Kingston's Kitchen & Grill. The police were thickest there, but with sheer brute force Atticus made his way through.

Before him was a bloody and brutal scene of carnage. At least a dozen bodies lined the slick red floor. Every one of the victims lay face down, their feet bound, their hands tied behind their back.

All the victims appeared to be from the neighbourhood, staff and customers alike. All were slain. Many Atticus didn't recognise. Some he did. The official greeter, Neville, was closest to the door, a hole in the back of his head where his life had been. It only took Atticus moments to find more familiar faces among the lifeless. Jacob, the cleaver-wielding kitchen hand, stared dead-eyed next to him. Nearby, Atticus's grandfather, Joe Wolfe, was flopped over his son, Thomas Wolfe—Atticus's father—as if in a last-ditch attempt to save the teenager's life. It had failed. Both men lay riddled with bullet holes.

The tears finally formed when Atticus saw his beloved grandmother, Eliza, her lifeless corpse prone in the corner, a bullet hole in the forehead of her once proud and beautiful face.

His family had been slaughtered.

Atticus stumbled out onto the street, police parting like the Red Sea, and threw up. Maggie was soon by his side, talking, but he didn't hear a single word. An incessant buzz echoed in his head, his sight blurred, and the world tilted before him. His limbs refused to work.

The only functional part of his body was his brain. He understood exactly what had happened. More than that, he knew who was responsible.

Perhaps he'd been spurred by Shelepin's assassination, perhaps not. In the end it was irrelevant.

Oliver had murdered Atticus's entire family.

FOURTEEN

TWELVE MONTHS IN THE FUTURE

Atticus cocooned himself away from the world for three straight days. He barely ate, barely drank, barely slept. If he did manage to drift off, he awoke with the fleeting hope that he'd had a nightmare, before realising it was nothing of the sort. It made falling asleep all the more difficult, knowing that when he awoke he'd have that brief glimmer of hope, only to be shattered once again. The pain of grief was all too real.

All the while, Maggie stayed by his side.

In the safe haven of Maggie's flat, immersed in his sorrow, Atticus picked up snippets from the outside world. The clandestine plan to assassinate Shelepin and blame members of his own party had spectacularly failed in every conceivable way.

Not only had the elite group of mainly SAS soldiers acted without authorisation, they had only mortally wounded Shelepin. The SAS team leader had been captured and, under torture, confessed all and was executed. Lingering in pain for days, the Soviet leader was conscious enough to plot his revenge. The world held its breath waiting for retaliation.

Floods of refugees fled every major city on the planet. Every available plane and ship was overstuffed with panicked citizens attempting to flee to anywhere they could. It was a refugee crisis like the world had never seen. They all realised what was coming. They all knew they couldn't outrun it. But they tried anyway.

While the world outside went mad, Maggie made sure that within the walls of her flat everything was calm and tranquil. Through the rough seas of his own grief with its monstrous peaks and troughs, Maggie was able to continually guide him back to shore. He loved her all the more for it.

The thing no one tells you about grief is its weight. Atticus felt heavy, weighed down by the heartache of losing his family all over again. The pain was so much harder to bear this time because he fully understood that it was all his fault. It may have been Oliver who had pulled the trigger, but it was Atticus who had loaded the gun.

In the darkest moments Atticus admitted to Maggie that he didn't know how he could live on knowing what he was responsible for. The loss he'd caused. And each time, Maggie shone her light, reminding him what was worth living for.

Managing to wrench himself from bed, have a shower and a shave, Atticus emerged from the bathroom wearing a towel and feeling marginally human for the first time in days. Maggie was putting on her coat.

"Was it something I said?"

Maggie's million dollar smile beamed. "Silly man. I'm off down the shops. They've mostly been stripped bare, but I'll see what I can scrounge. I'm sure Tilly has stashed away some essentials for the regulars."

"Let me guess, all the toilet paper is gone?"

"Yes!" She shook her head. "It was the first to go. Have you heard of anything so bizarre?"

Atticus chuckled. "I have, actually." He told Maggie about the early days of the Covid-19 pandemic and the rush on toilet paper. It seemed so trivial in relation to what was happening now, with the world on the brink of collapse. There was the very real possibility that the London he could see through the grubby windows of Maggie's flat would soon cease to exist. Its rich history, culture, its very life could evaporate at any moment.

"I'll be back in a few minutes. You'll be okay?"

"I will."

She kissed him. "Love you."

"Love you."

Atticus had just managed to get dressed when there was a knock at the door. He answered it with a grin on his face, suspecting Maggie had forgotten her key again. For such an intelligent and independent woman, she tended to forget her keys on a regular basis.

To the closed door, Atticus said, "I'm beginning to think we need to attach a keyring to your—"

But when Atticus yanked it open, there was no Maggie. There was no one at all. At the base of the stairs a male ran out into the street. From the way the figure moved, Atticus guessed it was a teenager. That was when he noticed the knife. Plunged into the door, it held an instant photograph in place. If Atticus was in another state of mind, he would have been surprised instant cameras existed this early. But

Atticus wasn't thinking about such trivial things. He was utterly focused on the subject of the photograph.

It was of an open car boot. Inside was a bound and gagged Maggie. The look of sheer terror in her eyes broke him. He should have been there. Atticus had been so caught up in his own grief he'd failed to protect the one thing that mattered most in the world.

With a shaking hand, he removed the photograph. On the other side was a handwritten address. He recognised it. He also knew the handwriting.

Atticus grabbed his coat and gun and sprinted into the street.

THE STREETS of London were in chaos.

Abandoned cars, personal possessions and clothing were strewn across empty streets littered with fluttering paper. Paddington was bereft of life, barring the stray cats and dogs that had emerged to fight over the last scraps of civilisation. Atticus sprinted alone through it all.

Passing a terrified group of youths clutching transistor radios, Atticus heard a newsman say, "I repeat, it is now believed both Moscow and New York have been hit. We have unconfirmed reports that Washington and Leningrad have also suffered nuclear strikes. We urge all citizens in the greater London area to evacuate..."

Most of the population had indeed fled. The few souls brave enough to step foot on the streets were either unwilling or unable to leave, darting from one side of the city to the other. Then, of course, there were the inevitable looters. On his way to Kensington Palace Green, Atticus witnessed a fight between groups pilfering from the abandoned upper-class neighbourhoods. Some were so organised they'd brought lorries. It was ridiculous to be fighting over the crumbs of a once great empire when all they might gain would soon be radioactive ash.

He was heading into a trap, of course. Atticus didn't care.

He would likely die. Atticus didn't care.

There was only one thing he cared for. Only one thing he would die for.

He forged on, the engagement ring bouncing in his pocket. Drained but resolute, he never once let his fatigue slow him. His mission was far too important.

As he rounded the corner, Atticus was shocked by the sight before him. He shouldn't have been, given the state of the rest of the city, but nonetheless he was taken by surprise. The vast and glorious Soviet embassy, the mammoth complex that stretched across the junction of Bayswater Road and Kensington Palace Gardens, stood abandoned. All seven of its gates were wide open. Stacks of files lay discarded by the roadside, as if jettisoned in a frenzied scramble to outrun the madness and destruction about to befall the city.

No guards manned the gates. There were no signs of life. The once steadfast and imposing symbol of the USSR's might and power sat discarded and forsaken. The hammer and sickle flag hung limply from a flagpole above the front doors, which were wide open.

Watching for movement for ten solid minutes, Atticus saw none. He tried to envisage the types of traps Oliver could have laid. He was certain there would be some. Oliver hadn't kidnapped the woman he loved to invite Atticus over for vodka and caviar.

If the staff had truly fled the embassy, Atticus would

have an advantage over the same scenario in the twenty-first century. There, motion and infrared detectors, CCTV cameras and the like would alert the entire complex that a breach had occurred. In this time, it all depended on human senses. And human senses could be fooled. That's what Atticus chose to exploit.

It took him only a few minutes to find the right partners for his endeavour. He spotted them lurking outside a high-walled estate. Atticus took a wild stab it wasn't their house, as they were struggling to haul a massive Granada Radiogram stereo cabinet down the street. How the four teenagers were meant to take the hulking thing anywhere without transport was beyond Atticus's understanding. By the dawning realisation on their faces, it seemed they were grappling with the same question.

Atticus approached slowly so as to not spook them. "Hey guys."

The shortest spun around in shock, leaving the others to bear the weight of the cabinet. The other three quickly lost equilibrium and the wooden console wabbled before crashing to the ground.

"Nice one, bruv. Look what ya made us do!"

The kids were all dressed as proto-rockers. Too young to be bikers, the slicked back hair, rolled up sleeves and plastered on sneers telecast exactly which cultural niche they aspired to. If they made it that far.

"Sorry about that." Atticus tried to be as non-threatening as possible. "How would you like to make a huge amount of money in a short amount of time?" He paused to gaze at the shattered pieces of the radiogram on the street. "And it won't be hard to cart away."

The youngest wiped his nose on his sleeve. "We're listening."

"See that building over there?"

"The Soviet Embassy?"

The kid knew the area. That was a bonus.

Atticus nodded to the kid. "That's the one. It's been abandoned, the guards and staff have fled."

"Yeah?" The kid was unimpressed. "What do I give a shit about files and blotters?"

"What's your name, kid?"

"Ken. Ken Nordli."

"Okay, Ken Nordli, do you care about diamonds?"

All four stood motionless, too stunned to offer an immediate response.

"What d'ya mean, diamonds?" Ken's face had morphed from cynical to hopeful in a matter of seconds.

"If you're British and secretly working for the Soviet Union, you don't exactly want to be paid in rubles, now do you?"

The kids regarded him blankly. He wasn't dealing with the sharpest knives in the block.

"Diamonds. Gold. English pounds. That's what the Soviets pay traitors with. It's all untraceable, don't you see?" The kids still had blank expressions on their faces, albeit more upbeat ones now. Atticus pointed. "And it's all in there, just beyond those unguarded walls."

Ken sniffed. "How d'you know all this?"

"Because it's my job to know these things." Atticus left the appropriate dramatic pause, then added, "I'm a spy."

"A black fucken spy? Get yer hand off it, mate."

"Would you suspect me of being a spy?"

The blinking and lack of response gave him his answer.

Atticus wasn't sure if it was his persuasive argument or their overwhelming greed, but once he laid out his plan, Ken's gang eagerly agreed. Atticus felt a slight amount of guilt that he may be subjecting the young quartet to undue risk at Oliver's hand, but at the same time, they were looting a dying city. Who knew, they might even find the treasure they sought.

They went over the plan in greater detail and synchronised their watches. The fact that they all possessed stolen Rolexes only reinforced Atticus's slight indifference to their fate.

Regardless, he issued them a warning. "At the first sign of anyone in there, get out. Make a racket on the way, but you don't want to mess with these people, you get me?"

Their nods affirmed they had heard. Whether they heeded his advice was another matter entirely.

The wait unfortunately gave Atticus pause, and his mind turned to darker thoughts. Was Maggie still even alive? Could he live without the woman he cared for more than anyone he had ever known? That disconsolate contemplation spiralled into visions of his murdered family, bound and slaughtered, bereft of their futures all because of one man's twisted thirst for vengeance. He'd soon learn what true vengeance meant.

At exactly three pm, Ken's team of four sprinted through the front entrance, making an almighty racket. Their target was a room on the third floor, the first on the right. For all Atticus know it could have been a toilet, but he'd convinced them it held riches beyond the dreams of avarice. Either way, they'd soon find out. Meanwhile, Atticus had other targets in mind.

Slipping through a window on the south side of the building, he found himself in the soldiers' commissary. It comprised racks of uniforms and boxes of supplies needed by the military personnel stationed at the embassy. Atticus smiled. He stripped down and got changed. It could give his adversary a moment's hesitation. In combat, sometimes that was enough to turn the tide of battle.

Moments later he emerged into the eerily quiet hallway of the Soviet embassy. Resplendent in his Red Army uniform, Atticus swung his newly acquired AK-47 at non-existent targets. Another three rifles were slung across his back.

The luxuriously carpeted stairs creaked beneath his feet, the sound reverberating about the empty stairwell. It truly did seem abandoned.

But Atticus knew better. Oliver wouldn't lure him to an empty building. He would only lure him to his doom.

As far as his adversary was concerned, Oliver had been stripped of everything he loved. Not only that, he'd hitched his ascension to a man who was now dead, and his hopes of ensuring a glorious Soviet Cold War victory lay in tatters.

As humanity slid into anarchy, even Oliver's smarts couldn't save him. The man truly had nothing left to live for, and a desperate man was a reckless and unpredictable one.

Considering that reckless and unpredictable man held the most precious thing Atticus had ever known, he appreciated the impossibility of what faced him. He didn't care.

The only thing that mattered was keeping Maggie safe. The world could go fuck itself for all Atticus cared. He had to save her. The nuclear furnace in his guts fired his very soul. Oliver was going to hell and Atticus was here to make sure he got there, even if he had to drag him there himself.

Atticus had been mad before. He'd been so incensed rational thought had seemed impossible. None of those times were comparable to the pure rage he now felt. Death itself would be incapable of keeping him from saving Maggie. He didn't need a reminder, but his hand delved into his pocket anyway, feeling the small felt box that contained the engagement ring. Atticus cracked his neck and ascended the stairs.

He tensed at a burst of gunfire, but it was in a distant part of the building, no doubt Ken Nordli and his cohorts discovering the embassy wasn't as abandoned as it had seemed. Using the diversion to his advantage, Atticus ran up the stairs.

The peaked cap of a Red Army soldier emerged from the stairway entry above him. The fresh-faced soldier made the fatal mistake of pausing when he saw Atticus, in uniform, advance on his position. It was the last mistake he ever made. Atticus's Kalashnikov barked once, and the soldier collapsed in a bloody heap.

Not waiting for any sign of retaliation, Atticus ran into the second-floor hallway. He should have waited. He faced a wall of Red Army soldiers, the eight military guards momentarily stunned by his sudden appearance.

Channelling the fury manifest in every atom he possessed, Atticus ran towards the mass of soldiers screaming like the madman he was, his AK-47 discharging a lethal flame of death. Without a backwards step, he rained fire on his enemy. The hail of bullets was unrelenting.

Bursts of red splattered their young bodies as Atticus sprinted towards them like some kind of demented hell-beast. When the assault rifle exhaled its last fiery breath he tossed it aside and unslung another. He advanced merci-lessly, not giving the terrified fighters a chance to counter-attack. His unyielding attack was cold-blooded in its efficiency.

Within seconds the steadfast Red Army soldiers lay dead, strewn across the floor in a smoking bloody mess. Except one. A bloodied private lay stunned, his shaking hand slick with the blood of his comrades. Atticus stepped towards him, discarding the last of his spent assault rifles. He extracted his pistol and fired a bullet between the young man's eyes.

Atticus had no time for mercy.

He marched on.

In the centre of the second floor, a large set of double doors were protected by two nervous soldiers sheltering behind an upturned desk. Sprawled on the hallway floor was the slain body of Ken Nordli. The poor kid hadn't heeded his advice. It was a shame, but Atticus was too laser focused to lament the kid's passing right now.

It was obvious from the look on their terrified faces the soldiers had heard the horror that had been rained down on their comrades and were petrified by the ruthless spectre. The same horror now advanced on their feebly constructed barricade.

It only took four bullets to remove the human obstruction. Atticus dragged the two dead soldiers aside, picked up two AK-47s and kicked open the doors.

Oliver spun, gun in hand. A massive grandiose chandelier hung above the beautifully polished parquet floor of the ballroom. But Atticus wasn't here for the aesthetics.

Maggie sat on a hard wooden chair, strapped into place. She appeared unharmed. Her mouth dropped open when he burst in.

"My god, Atticus." Her voice hitched. "What happened to you?"

Atticus swivelled to Oliver. "He did."

With a Makarov pistol pressed into the side of Maggie's head, Oliver said, "Drop your weapons. You know what will happen if you don't."

Atticus's assault weapons clattered to the wooden floor.

It was a calculated gamble. Knowing Oliver as he did, their history, their confrontations, he knew his opponent would want one last gloat, one last speech. Atticus was counting on it. He stood open handed, palms out to show Oliver he posed no immediate threat. The two men scowled at one another.

In the distance, the screeching roar of air raid sirens broke the uncomfortable silence. London's early warning system alerted citizens that missiles were on their way. Atticus didn't care about what was happening outside, only what was transpiring within this room.

Atticus's bearing changed when he turned to Maggie. "Hey, beautiful. How are you?"

Her glance shifted between the gun held to her head then the window letting in the warning siren, then to Atticus. "I'm not going to lie, I've had better days."

Oliver looked behind Atticus, confused. "Where... where's the rest of them? I assumed you'd bring a brigade of Gurkhas with you."

Atticus took a step forward, but Oliver pressed his pistol harder into Maggie's temple and shook his head. It took all his self-control to manage the power of speech. "I don't need an army." He motioned to Maggie. "I just need her." He turned to the man he once considered a friend. "You've brought chaos on the world, Oliver. It's time to stop. There's nothing for you to gain here. It's over, for everyone. Just let her go, please."

There were screams outside now, at the sudden realisation of what the sirens meant.

"Why are you doing this, Oliver? Maggie was your friend once."

Oliver chuckled, his pupils like plates. The man was on

some sort of drug, which only added to his unhinged demeanour.

Her words cracked and brittle, Maggie said, "Go. Please just go, Atticus. I need you to live."

It broke his heart to see her like this. A million men with a million chains couldn't drag Atticus away from Maggie. He'd killed to get to her. A literal murder spree. His violence was normally reserved, maiming where he could, always erring on the side of being merciful. But not now. Not for her. He was willing to kill everyone on the planet just to see her safe.

"You're about to die, Atticus Wolfe." Oliver gestured indifferently to the noise outside. "Well, we all are, but I'd be damned if I didn't get to see it myself." He let out a maniacal laugh. "Nuclear bombs are so impersonal, don't you think?" His glassy eyes widened. "I want to see the expression on your face when your pitiful life leaves your body. I want to see you die, Atticus Wolfe."

"You've got one sick fetish, Oliver."

Atticus glanced around the room in search of a distraction, a way to gain the upper hand. There was no doubt he was going to kill Oliver, he just had to be sure Maggie was safe first.

"I've got you, Atticus Wolfe." Oliver practically jumped, like an excited child. "I finally have you!"

"Why do you keep saying my full name? It makes you sound even more deranged than you already are."

Waving a dismissive hand, Oliver's drug-addled eyes widened once more. "I'm not unhinged, I'm brilliant."

"Although not modest, apparently."

Oliver shook his head, still holding the gun to Maggie's temple. "Look how far I've gotten without the great and all-knowing Atticus Wolfe. You've seen all the things I've achieved. I fooled all of MI6. Nobody saw what I truly was."

"I wouldn't say nobody."

Oliver ignored Atticus's quip; he was too deep into his unhinged rant. "Then after your treachery I soared in the Soviet ranks, becoming one of the most powerful men on the planet. A king maker. I was reshaping the world. I would have, too, if not for your incompetent interference." He waved a hand at the window. "I did all that, *I* achieved all these things without you. You have to admit you're impressed, aren't you Atticus Wolfe?"

There was an expectant pause from Oliver and he leaned forward, awaiting a reply.

"All this," Atticus shook his head in surprise, "everything you've done, the destruction you've wrought... you're trying to impress me?"

In his current state, it took a lot to penetrate Atticus's focused anger, but that statement did it. Maggie was completely right. Oliver was in some kind of twisted love with Atticus.

He had minutes to get Maggie to safety. He had to speed things along.

"Fine. Yes, I'm impressed, Oliver. You actually have achieved so much in such a short amount of time."

Outside, the sirens continued their mournful warning wail.

"But by the sounds of it, you don't have much time to enjoy it." Atticus's free hand flexed. "Let her go and you can do whatever you want with me."

The choice of words was deliberate. Maggie noticed it too.

"You'd say anything to save her." With his free hand, Oliver waggled a finger at Atticus. He wiped drool from the corner of his mouth with his sleeve, his glazed eyes becoming more unfocused by the minute. "She's just going to distract you. Here, let me fix that."

Oliver pulled the trigger.

Atticus's world ended.

Maggie, the woman who meant more than he had once believed possible, slumped in the chair, her beautiful eyes no longer sparked with life.

Oliver spun towards Atticus, seemingly shocked at what he'd done. Unthinking, Atticus extracted the two pistols he'd taken from the guards outside the boardroom and fired them simultaneously. The first two shots hit Oliver dead in the centre in his heart. The next were headshots. Even as Oliver's lifeless body fell, Atticus continued to fire, pummelling Oliver again and again, shot after shot. He walked forward, still firing even after Oliver hit the floor. When the pistols were spent, he picked up his discarded assault weapons and continued to fire until they too were exhausted. His finger continued pulling the trigger even though there were no more bullets to give.

Finally, Atticus let go of his weapons and collapsed at Maggie's feet. Untying her gently, he lay her on the ground, holding her close for an eternity and no time at all. Time no longer had any meaning.

Time.

Time.

The light outside steadily grew darker. The sirens continued their wail. Life went on. At least, for a short while.

It took every ounce of strength Atticus had to stand. Tears still flowing, he staggered towards the door.

He'd failed Maggie. He'd been unable to save the most

important person he'd ever known. She was dead because of him.

But he could still save her.

Somehow, Atticus managed to make his legs move. More than move, run. And once he began, he couldn't stop.

OUT OF BREATH, Atticus used the last ounce of strength he had to knock on the door. It swung open to reveal a surprised Ganim.

"Jesus, what the hell happened to—"

Atticus pushed past him into his flat. Inside was a mess. Cables and computer parts were strewn across Atticus's once pristine home. They'd relocated the prototype when the other scientists started to sniff around, suspecting that the computer they'd been working on wasn't designed to detect incoming missiles at all.

Stripped down to its essential components, the Frankenstein monster of a computer was roughly twice the size of Atticus's couch. Connected to Atticus's mobile phone and Ganim's keypad, it was the backup they all hoped they'd never need.

The other man shut the door and looked Atticus up and down. "Nice uniform. Bit early for Halloween, don't you think?" All levity ended when Ganim saw Atticus's face. "Good lord, what happened?"

Staggering to the armchair, Atticus dropped the AK-47 from his wearied hands and fell into the seat. In the few words he could muster, Atticus told him what Oliver had done, both to his family and Maggie.

Too shocked for words, Ganim remained silent, coming to grips with what had happened. Then, instead of consoling him, Ganim sprang up and pulled a lever. The whole room erupted in a cacophony of mechanical sounds, finally managing to drown out the sirens.

"Seems like we'll be needing this backup after all." Ganim turned to Atticus. "We haven't tested this. Are you sure?"

Atticus nodded. He literally had nothing left to lose.

The phone rang but Atticus couldn't muster the energy to move. He ignored it.

"Have you heard? Half the eastern seaboard in the US is gone. All the big cities too. No idea why we haven't been hit yet." He flicked his thumb to the noisy window. "Though I think our luck's run out. Berlin, Paris..." Receiving no response from Atticus, Ganim went back to tinkering with the great machine. "This is the end of days. They wanted you back at work." He nodded to the phone. "That was probably MI6 again. They keep calling, wanting you back at work." His laugh was bitter. "As if that's going to help. This will." He slapped the great machine. "I'm sorry about Maggie. And your family. I can't imagine..."

Ganim kept talking but Atticus had stopped listening. Both his tiny little world and the larger world were ending. He found it impossible to find an emotion to land on, though grief was generating the most gravity. All he could see was Maggie's slain form. The one he'd abandoned on a dirty floor in a deserted building. He felt sick to his core that he'd left her there, but he couldn't stay.

Sitting there in his flat, Atticus's mind screamed to just give up, to lay down and wait for the bombs. But he couldn't. Not when there was still a chance to save her.

He stood unsteadily and slung the AK-47 over his back. He had no idea how much time had passed since Ganim started fiddling with his great machine. Finally, he turned to Atticus and gave him the thumbs up.

Staggering forward, Atticus stood near Ganim's machine and tried to prepare for what he had to do should the scientist actually pull this off. He couldn't go through what he'd just experienced again. If he truly was to meet his past self, then he never wanted that Atticus to feel the unending loss that would torment his soul forever. He had to succeed. Literally everything rested on it.

Flicking the final switch, Ganim's machine emitted a high-pitched whine. The ends of the electric rods sparked, creating a churning green vapour. The machine grew louder, the swirling vortex expanding with every octave. The windows shook.

There was no denying the glee on Ganim's face as he watched the sparking whirlpool form. On seeing Atticus his expression darkened, as if he was embarrassed to have been caught taking joy in his achievement.

Atticus gave him a grim smile to tell him it was okay, and received a po-faced nod of encouragement in reply.

Ganim picked up a wad of papers from the desk and stuffed them into Atticus's hand. "You might need these. They're the complete plans. Everything I'd need just in case... in case it's needed again."

Atticus gazed down at the technical plans and shook his head in confusion. "You're not coming?"

"No. Not this time." Ganim tried to sound more resolute than he appeared. "Don't reveal too much about the future, alright? Just the bare minimum. Giving them too much could alter things badly."

They gazed out the window, then back at each other, and smiled. Gallows humour.

Ganim went on. "Alright, badly in other ways. Just keep

to the bare essentials—enough to know what they're up against, but not enough to freak them out." He patted Atticus on the shoulder. "Now go, my friend."

"Come with me, we can both—"

Ganim shook his head once more. "One man is going to mess things up enough. Two—well, that would be too much for the timeline to take, I suspect."

Atticus looked outside. He couldn't see any missiles, but he knew they were on the way. "But you'll die."

"Not if you do your job." Ganim pulled the handle and the swirling, sparking maelstrom doubled in size. "Be safe, my friend. You have to go. Now."

Taking a deep inhale, Atticus forced himself to believe he could stop all this from happening. He had to.

As he gave the old man a grin of thanks, a great flash engulfed everything. For a fleeting instant, the entire world was blindingly white. Outside the huge windows of his Covent Garden flat, a giant mushroom cloud formed somewhere in the north of London.

Atticus stepped into the vortex.

FIFTEEN

BACK TO TWELVE MONTHS BEFORE

"And the rest, you know." Older Atticus's hand shook as he reached for a glass of water.

They stared at him in stunned silence.

"The fuck did you just tell us?"

Ganim's words manifested what the rest of the room was collectively thinking. Rathdowne, Ganim, Maggie and the two Atticuses sat huddled together in stunned silence.

"London was bombed?" Rathdowne swallowed hard. "Nuclear bombed?"

Older Atticus smoothed out his in-progress beard and held up a hand before Rathdowne could question him further. "Like I said, knowing too much could jeopardise what's meant to unfold in unforeseen ways. Hell, I've seen firsthand what happens when just one man sees the future, and his actions condemned the whole damned world. I *had* to be the lone holder of this information, but you just kept at me and at me. Are you happy now? Do you feel better?" There was a bitterness to his words. "No, I didn't think so. Now you have to live with what I know. Well done, you've all heard the whole fucking awful truth."

The bulk of his anger was directed at his younger self, as if it were all his fault. And in a way it was, of course. After all, they were the ones responsible for messing up the timeline in the first place.

It made a lot more sense now. The lingering gazes at Maggie, all of it. Not only had he lost the woman he loved at the hand of a madman, but he'd seen her materialise before his eyes soon after, only to realise she wasn't his. For a moment Atticus tried to imagine what that was like for the older Atticus. To see the person he loved most in the world every day, only for her to be in the arms of another man. The fact that man was himself would hardly matter.

"But why would he hold Miss Dunbar hostage like that?"

Everyone else rolled their eyes at Rathdowne's question. It seemed he was destined to remain ignorant about their romance. Evidently, the man's perceptiveness was confined to espionage.

Younger Atticus folded his arms. "I get what you're saying about trying not to mess things up further, but this information would have been handy when I confronted Oliver in Moscow. To tell him how far everything went."

Shaking his head, Older Atticus said, "The man I saw in that embassy was utterly unhinged. That twisted soul lives somewhere inside the present Oliver. How deep inside, I have no idea, but he's there. That deranged creature wouldn't care about the semantic difference between one nuked city or a hundred. I'm pretty sure the present one wouldn't either. The only way to stop Oliver is to kill him, like I've been saying since the start. That's our next step. If anyone wants to argue, let's have it."

No one argued.

"The people in this room are the only ones able to prevent the future we've just heard about." Younger Atticus was less dubious of his other self now he knew the whole story. "If we take stupid risks no one here will survive, and everyone else will die with us. We have to be precise. We have to be prepared to do whatever it takes."

The group made plans to create additional teams to track down Oliver. So far their efforts had gone unrewarded, the man having disappeared after the confrontation in Moscow. They hoped his luck wouldn't hold. Sooner or later he'd have to surface somewhere. They hoped for the former.

The meeting wrapped up and everyone went their separate ways. As Younger Atticus walked out with Maggie, he saw the lingering gaze they received from his other self. For the first time, he fully understood it.

YOUNGER ATTICUS SPUN on his chair, staring at the ceiling. "What if..." he continued his whirling. "What if...?"

Maggie, Younger and Older Atticus had been cooped up in their office for the better part of a day. They'd been debating the same subject MI6 had been focused on in the week and a half since the confrontation in Moscow—finding Oliver.

So far the only thing the three of them had discovered was how awkward they felt around each other. Even more than before. Relations had already been strained, but that had significantly ramped up since he'd divulged the rest of his story. A day in close proximity hadn't helped matters.

Maggie sat at a long wooden table, and Older Atticus sat at the end of it. Whether it was deliberate or not, Maggie had made a fort of folders, separating the two of them.

"What if," Younger Atticus continued his chair whirling, "we're going about this all wrong?"

"How are you not dizzy?" Maggie asked over a cup of tea.

"Oh, I am." Younger Atticus spun. "I think there's another way we can approach this. We've been trying to search for a man who doesn't want to be found. In fact, I bet he's vying for the Guinness Book of Records hide-and-seek championship."

"I think he's spin crazy." Older Atticus spoke up. He'd been quiet for most of the day, seemingly hoping the others would forget he existed. There was no chance of that.

Atticus continued his whirling. "You don't catch a rabbit by waiting for it to poke its head out of its burrow."

"Is this going to be a Bugs Bunny metaphor?"

Ignoring Maggie's taunt, Younger Atticus went on. "You set a trap. But that's not enough. You have to entice it out of its safe, cosy hiding place. You have to give it something it wants."

"We're going to lure Oliver out with some soggy lettuce?" Older Atticus's tone was sarcastic. He sat up, suddenly annoyed. "Will you stop spinning!"

"No." Younger Atticus spun some more. "So instead of us trying to find Oliver, we need to offer him what he wants to lure him out of his hidey hole. Something he can't refuse."

"Like what?"

"I hadn't got that far." Younger Atticus twirled on. "I don't know. A really nice cookie? Like, crisp on the outside but nice and gooey in the centre."

Older Atticus grunted.

"I'm really fucking dizzy here."

Giggling, Maggie suggested, "Then stop spinning."

"I don't think I can."

Amused, Maggie walked over to stop Younger Atticus's chair. He held up a finger as the world continued to spin. Eventually it slowed down enough for him to stand, albeit unsteadily.

"I might go lie down for a bit."

Younger Atticus swayed out the door, leaving Maggie and Older Atticus alone for the first time. Watching him go, Maggie chuckled and shook her head. As she turned, she caught a glimpse of Older Atticus watching her. It was the kind of doe-eyed gaze she'd learned to ignore. Eyes darting back to his report, Older Atticus did his best to pretend he hadn't been staring. Neither of them bought it.

Maggie made her way back to the table. Without glancing up, she spoke softly. "I get it now."

Pretending to be engrossed in a CIA report on the list of Soviet officials for Brezhnev's upcoming trip to Ghana, Older Atticus raised his head. "What's that?"

"I get it." Her voice was full of sympathy. "After hearing your story, I understand now. That's why you look at me the way you do. Your Maggie died."

Older Atticus moved a folder aside and placed his hand on top of hers. "You're my Maggie."

Gently, without sudden movement, she moved his hand away. "No, I'm not." Maggie tilted her head compassion-ately, but her words were strong. "This whole time travel thing is messed up for everyone, you in particular. There's no victor here, no one wins. I honestly can't comprehend just how tough this must be for you, but I'm guessing it's close to torture. I want you to know I understand." She gently reached out to touch his arm before withdrawing her hand again. "But the man who just walked out, the dizzy stupid one, he's *my* Atticus. There can be only one, and he's mine. I'm so sorry, truly sorry, but it has to be him."

Older Atticus nodded, as if he'd been expecting the answer. "I tried, Maggie, I really did." His eyes were watery. "I tried to keep my distance, to be respectful. I tried to rationalise it, to tell myself *he*," Older Atticus waved to the door, "was yours and I was the useless third wheel. I *tried* to stop loving you, I really did, but that's utterly impossible. You are the most amazing woman I've ever known, the only one who's truly seen me, the one I gave my entire heart to." He swallowed hard. "The one I can't live without."

Shifting in her chair, Maggie straightened her back slightly. "There will be others." She held up her hand. "That sounded like a clichéd reflex answer, but it's not. You will find love again, Atticus, I know you will. But I have to say this again, just to be absolutely clear because uncertainty isn't fair. Atticus, my Atticus, the one I met here in my timeline, he's the one for me. He always will be. Do you understand what I'm saying?"

Face contorted with pain, Older Atticus moved his hand closer to hers, but didn't touch her. "But don't you see? I love you more than he does. I've known you longer, we have more of history, a greater bond. We were together longer. Hell, we were going to get married."

That made Maggie sit up. "We were?"

He bobbed his head enthusiastically. "I even bought a ring. I was all set to propose when..." His face darkened. "If anything, I deserve you more because I love you more. I know you better." He inhaled unsteadily. "Every time I'm in the same room as you and I can't touch you a piece of me falls away. I'm no longer whole." He swallowed hard. "I don't know if I can live without you, Maggie. I need you like oxygen."

For a long time they sat in silence. Having said his piece, Atticus was still, letting her process his words. Maggie on the other hand sat, head downcast and lips pursed. Eventually she raised her head.

"I'm sorry, but it's still no." She moved on quickly in case there was a protest. "I love Atticus—and by extension, that means you, of course, you're the same person in most respects. But I have to state this again. My Atticus, the one I love more than life itself and want to spend the rest of my life with, is through that door. There can't be any ambiguity on that, no hidden hope that may change, because it won't. I honestly never want to hurt you, Atticus, truly, you've obviously been through so much. You don't deserve this, any of it, but it's the way it had to be. *Will* be. My choice is him. It always will be. I hope you can understand that, if not now, then some day."

Face crumbling, Atticus's eyes grew strained. "But I know what it's like to lose you. I don't know if I can do that a second time." He went to hold her hand, but Maggie drew hers back before he made contact. "But I will do my best." There was defeat on his face now.

"I come bearing Rathdownes!"

Younger Atticus strode through the office door, his boss trailing, annoyed, behind him. Once he'd entered the room, Younger Atticus glanced between his other self and Maggie, sensing something was up. He tilted his head inquisitively at Maggie and she gave a flick of her head as if to say, *I'll tell you later.*

"Dunbar. Wolfe." Rathdowne shook his head. "I still can't get used to repeating myself around you two." He turned to Maggie. "I don't know how you cope with two of them all the time, Dunbar."

Maggie cast s fleeting look towards Older Atticus. "It's a work in progress."

Rathdowne sat at the table with a thud. "Alright, what have you lot come up with?"

"We've spun up a scenario." Younger Atticus was clearly amused by his choice of words. "Instead of looking under every rock in the Soviet Union, we entice Oliver out of hiding. Give him a carrot he can't resist, an inducement to raise his head above the parapet."

Grunting his approval, Rathdowne said, "Alright, makes sense. So what is this grand incentive you've cooked up to get him out of the trenches?"

"Ah, that's thing," Younger Atticus scratched the back of his neck, "we haven't got to that part of the plan yet."

Rathdowne's frown migrated from approving to his usual default of unimpressed. "Hardly a robust and well thought-through blueprint for success. I think you lot need to—"

"I know what will get Oliver out of hiding."

All heads turned to Older Atticus. His body seemed deflated, smaller than before.

"What if we give Oliver exactly what he wants?" Older Atticus tapped the report he'd been reading as he gazed forlornly at Maggie. "What if we give him me?"

CHAPTER
SIXTEEN

"This is the most ludicrous plan I've ever heard of in my life." Josef Oduwo, head of MI6 West African operations, shook his head.

"Joseph," Younger Atticus patted the big man on the shoulder, "ask Cohen about the two other missions he's been on with me." Atticus stretched his arms above his head. "He'll tell you about ludicrous."

Oduwo grimaced and his gaze drifted off, as if he were imagining a scenario more absurd than what he'd been thrust in the middle of.

Through their earpieces, Cohen responded, "Yeah, I can attest those missions were completely bonkers, mate." There was a slight pause before he added, "But I have to agree with you, this one is extra tonto."

Younger Atticus and Oduwo sat on rickety chairs at front of a rickety table in front of an equally rickety bar. They sat under an umbrella nursing warm bottles of Pepsi, facing the bustling street of Accra, Ghana. The scene pulsated with locals going about their late afternoon business, oblivious to the tense espionage play taking place in their midst.

Further up the road, Cohen, Maggie and Older Atticus sat in an open Jeep in the main street of Accra's Jamestown. Everyone wore shorts and short-sleeved shirts. Everyone but Oduwo was sweating, with the temperature in the high nineties.

The air smelt strongly of the sea drifting in from the nearby Atlantic, mixed with the heady scent of deep-fried seafood from the countless nearby restaurants. The streets were crowded with shoppers buying bright clothing, groceries and jewellery. Their cheerful chatter mixed with the loud live music, adding to the vibrant atmosphere. High above the low rooftops stood a red-and-white lighthouse, a relic of the era of slavery and British colonial rule.

If circumstances were different, Younger Atticus would have enjoyed the atmosphere and immersed himself in the pulsating street life. Unfortunately he had no such luxury. They were on the deadliest of missions.

It all started when Older Atticus had read the report on Brezhnev's upcoming trip to Ghana. The list of officials attending also included Shelepin, which automatically piqued his attention. The report named the entire thirty-strong entourage, bar one individual who was listed as "Shelepin Aid". That was enough to set the machine in motion.

They asked the head of the West African office, Oduwo, to use his connections to find who this mysterious unnamed person was. The irony wasn't lost on Atticus that when he'd first started at MI6 in this time period, Rathdowne had tried to force him to join the African bureau. That moment felt like a million years ago.

Fortuitously, Cohen had been in-country working with

Oduwo for six months assessing the rising Soviet influence in Ghana. Their investigation of Brezhnev's trip resulted in an equally Oliver-shaped hole from their end. While the accommodation requests had roles assigned for all thirty delegates, Cohen discovered there were two separate hotel room reservations under Shelepin's name. It was too much of a coincidence. They booked flights immediately.

They'd arrived the night before and were warmly greeted by a beaming Cohen. He'd shown them around, set them up in a hotel and helped refine their plan. Snatching Oliver when he was—probably—part of an official Soviet delegation was not without its challenges. One wrong move would mean international disaster and would shore up the kind of future they were actively trying to prevent.

After two and a half hours sitting under the straw umbrella, Oduwo and Atticus were running out of things to talk about.

"This plan is foolhardy." Oduwo shook his head.

"You're one to talk. You just used 'foolhardy' in a sentence." Atticus sipped his drink.

"I doubt London would have approved this." He frowned. "It's hardy following the rules."

Atticus was forced to match the other man's frown in agreeance. "Rules are made for the guidance of wise men and the obedience of fools."

Oduwo turned to Atticus. "That's a good quote." His face broke into a smile for the first time since they'd sat down. "I've heard it somewhere before but I can't quite place it."

"Sir Douglas Robert Steuart Bader." Atticus stretched. "Postscript, Bader lost his legs disobeying the rules."

Oduwo's smile evaporated. "That, uh, is less encouraging." He went back to his scowling.

None of the MI6 team were officially there. Given Ghana had gained its independence from Britain some seven years previously, the current administration wouldn't be too receptive to their presence. Still officially part of the Commonwealth, the relationship between the two nations was strained. In recent years Ghana had flirted with communism and had forged closer ties with the USSR.

In a few short years Ghana's first president, Kwame Nkrumah, would be overthrown in a coup d'état. For now, though, he was playing East against West to garner the best deal for his country. Which was why Brezhnev was on his way. It would be one of the first trips the new leader had made overseas. The Soviets were eager to convert the world to their cause and saw Africa as ripe for indoctrination. In Atticus's recollection it never amounted to much, but for a short time Moscow and the West each scrambled to exert their ideological influence over newly independent colonies.

Nkrumah referred to himself as the African Lenin, but so far he'd failed to live up to that moniker. Even within Ghana the socialists were fractured. There were several communist factions vying for supremacy. The Ghanaian Communist Party. The United Party of Communist Ghana. The Socialist Alliance. The Popular Ghanaian Front. Atticus found it amusing that the latter had only eleven members. They all wanted to be on top of the pile if the country became a puppet state of the Soviets, the first in Africa, an honour that would no doubt bring an influx of funds and with that, privilege. The old "some are more equal than others" adage.

Brezhnev would do his best to secure a Ghanian future under the hammer and sickle; he was scheduled to arrive the next day. Many of the officials had already landed, preparing for the welcome ceremony and ensuring a smooth and successful visit. The Oliver-shaped hole was among them.

If the mysterious entourage member was indeed Oliver, he may feel safer in Africa, far from Europe and MI6's sphere of influence. Younger Atticus found it ironic that Oliver felt safer in a country where his skin colour didn't exactly blend in with the population. That was, if he was in Ghana at all. They had contingencies if he wasn't, but they were gambling he was.

Which was why Younger Atticus and Oduwo were casually sipping lukewarm Pepsis and pretending to take in the scenery. The bar was a notorious Soviet meeting point.

Since Oduwo had been frequenting Ghana for years, he was well known to the local Soviets as an MI6 agent. That was why he used people like Cohen, who were unknown to the locals. By merely sitting with him, Younger Atticus was drawing attention to himself.

Add to that, over the last few months Oduwo and Cohen had observed countless meetings at the same bar between known KGB agents and representatives of the Ghana government and local authorities. The staff were confirmed to be on the Soviet payroll. Given his encounter in Moscow, Atticus had no doubt he'd be a known presence throughout the KGB network. In fact, he was counting on it.

Since they'd arrived, both men had spoken openly of Brezhnev, MI6 and the KGB. Oduwo had waited until the owner, the local branch leader of the Ghanaian Communist Party in Accra, was nearby and then loudly asked, "Who the hell do you think you are, Atticus Wolfe?"

Now they just had to wait.

Older Atticus had lobbied hard to be the bait instead of his slightly younger self. He hadn't gotten his way. Younger

Atticus understood the rage his counterpart must have felt, but knew it could very well compromise the mission. The man was too emotionally raw to face off against Oliver. His anger made him unpredictable. Dangerous. For a mission this critical, it was too much of a risk. At the same time, Younger Atticus knew he would be exactly the same if someone had slayed *his* family, had murdered *his* Maggie before his eyes.

"How reliable is your team?" Oduwo's words roused Younger Atticus from his meandering thoughts. "Can they be counted on in a pinch?"

Younger Atticus smiled. "They're the best there is."

"But the woman..."

"Is more capable than any agent I've ever known."

"If that's what you believe, then fine, but if we get into a scrape, perhaps it's best that she—"

"She's been involved in more scrapes, as you put it, than most agents at MI6. Believe me, I've seen her handle situations that would have caused lesser agents to run."

"But surely she's better off—"

"Uh, fellas?" Cohen's voice crackled in their earpieces. "Did you forget we can hear you?"

The rapid descent of Oduwo's jaw indicated he had indeed forgotten. Not so his companion.

"Not at all, mate." Younger Atticus raised his eyebrows at Oduwo.

"The woman," Maggie's voice cut through the air like a sword, "is ready and waiting, and more than willing to show anyone who cares to observe just what she's capable of."

Atticus couldn't help but grin. Oduwo on the other hand, shrunk. While his attitude was all too common in the sixties, it had been a while since Atticus had heard such blatant sexism. At head office, Maggie had earned the respect, albeit grudgingly, of her peers by simply outperforming them. By the end of the mission he had no doubt Oduwo would see just how skilled Maggie Dunbar was.

Silence descended as they waited for their plan to play out. The sun was setting and restaurants were pulling out their awnings, preparing for the night-time bustle.

Even by Atticus's standards, the plan they had created was complicated. It had been designed in to mitigate the chances of MI6 being held accountable for the loss of Oliver. Though, Atticus had to admit, the chances were still higher than he'd like.

First step, let the KGB know Atticus was in-country. Given their current activity, he was reasonably confident that had been achieved. Second, have one of the communist factions—surreptitiously on the payroll of MI6—publicly kidnap Atticus from the bar in less than an hour.

Two hours following that, the communist captors would contact their communist associates to advise they had been raided by *another* unknown faction who had kidnapped Atticus from them. The scene would be staged with bullet holes, blood and broken furniture. The faked kidnapping of Atticus would create confusion and raise tensions. It would also absolve the United Party of Communist Ghana of suspicion and allow them to remain in the pocket of MI6.

The final piece was the trickiest. They would get word to Oliver that Atticus was being held captive by a hitherto unknown communist faction. They would ask Oliver to come alone. With a ransom. Which was very un-communist, but Atticus assumed even communists had to eat. And then they would take down Oliver once and for all.

The whole scenario would play into the KGB's very

nature. They were all about subtlety and subterfuge, not overt acts of aggression. Even if they suspected MI6 involvement in Oliver's disappearance, the Soviets had little sway in the country, despite Brezhnev's visit. Still closely tied to their former colonial masters, Ghana was just starting to find its own voice. Most of the country was not in the thrall of communism, nor was the sentiment completely anti-British. The Soviets would need to tread lightly if they wanted Ghana to be the first Soviet domino to fall in Africa. It was a balancing act for all.

Oduwo assured them he had the right people in place to make it work. The plan rested on his shoulders, in more ways than one.

Younger Atticus heard the screeching tyres first. Glancing up, he saw pedestrians dart in all directions to escape the three white Dodge A100 vans hurtling towards them. The vans skidded to a halt in front of the bar.

Oduwo's head snapped around to Atticus's, fear darkening his eyes. "These are not my men."

Further down the road, popping sounds reverberated off the surrounding buildings. Gunfire.

"Atticus, we're under fi—"

He tapped his earpiece, Oduwo did the same. The latter turned to him and despondently shook his head. His line had gone dead too.

They'd been ambushed. Ten burly men dressed as Ghanaian police poured out of the unmarked vans. Nearby civilians screamed and scrambled out of their way. Their clubs suggested they were disinclined to confirm if they were real police or not. Atticus doubted he'd get the chance to ask. As soon as they cleared the vans, all ten ran at the pair.

Oduwo stood and took the first swing. He connected

with the jaw of the first cop, but the second beat him down. Atticus was marginally more successful, managing to collect a couple of good jabs, but the men soon enveloped him, mercilessly pounding him with truncheons. Forced to curl into a ball, Atticus protected his head and contorted with pain as the cops pummelled him without mercy.

Atticus was unsure how long the battering lasted, but eventually a bag was thrust over his head. A group of cops manhandled him into one of the vans and sped off. Disoriented, Younger Atticus had no idea who was in the van or the fate of his team or Oduwo. Every time he moved or attempted to speak, another blow was the only response.

He tasted blood and one tooth wobbled. Without being able to feel them with his hands he guessed at least one rib was bruised, possibly broken.

The van bumped over rough roads for at least fifteen minutes before slowing to a halt. Multiple shouts intersected in a cacophony of noise. Atticus couldn't understand the local dialect but assumed the information being conveyed wasn't which five-star resort room was his. Among the idling van and overlapping orders he could make out the roar of a different kind of engine. Jet engines. They were near the airport.

"Guys, look, this is really embarrassing, but I left my passport back at the hotel."

Atticus collected a punch to the stomach in reply. It was a good one; it knocked the wind out of him so much he wondered if he'd draw another breath. He was wrenched from the van and dragged at least thirty metres to a building of some sort, then down a series of corridors. He was finally thrown into a room, handcuffed to a chair and punched once more for good measure before finally having his hood yanked away.

Eyes adjusting to the dazzling light, it took a few moments for his vision to return. The stark room was bereft of any furnishing except two chairs. Atticus sat on one. The one opposite him was also occupied.

Atticus grinned a bloody grin. "Hello, Oliver."

"You really have outdone yourself, haven't you?"

"Thank you." Atticus's head was ringing from the beating. "What for this time?"

Oliver pushed back his glasses. "Following me all the way to Africa. If circumstances were different I'd almost say I was flattered."

Atticus tested his restraints, but they held fast. Unfortunately. Oliver opened his jacket and revealed the grip of a pistol, just to remind Atticus who was in charge.

"How about you undo these and we just hug it out? What do you say?"

"Do you think I'm stupid?"

Younger Atticus asked, "I don't think you want me to answer that honestly, do you?"

Oliver didn't reply. Instead, he pulled a pack of cigarettes from his suit pocket and lit one. It was pure theatrics; Oliver wasn't much of a smoker. The slight cough he desperately tried to cover conveyed as much.

"I thought about what you told me, about the nuclear bombs and such." He waved his cigarette about. "The more I thought about it, the more insane it seemed. I mean, how on earth would you be able to come by that information? And if you could, I would hardly be your target." He shook his head. "Though try as I might, I haven't been able to come up with your angle. I just can't fathom why you would come all the way to Moscow with some asinine science fiction story, nor what you expected me to do with it. That still has me stumped."

Atticus gave him a nonplussed expression. There was no changing the man's mind, so why bother?

"What happens to me now?"

A sinister chuckle escaped Oliver's thin lips. "You'll be hauled back to Moscow in one of our official planes. I'm sure I can requisition one for a short stint and return it before the State work here is done." He raised an eyebrow. "Once you're behind the Iron Curtain your experience won't be... pleasant, I hate to inform you."

"Do you though?"

"No." The smile didn't leave his face. "No, I don't." Oliver leaned forward. "That's why I insisted on the police chief bringing you to the airport. I don't want to risk a last-minute reprieve by your so-called friends. I'm shipping you out in a few minutes. When you arrive, the KGB will want their pound of flesh, of course, extracting all they can from that tiny little mind of yours. Then, when you've been thoroughly broken down, I'll take over, extracting all the information about the future I could possibly use to shape history as it should transpire."

"And then? I suppose a week in Bali at a yoga retreat is out of the question?"

Oliver sighed in annoyance. "After that, I haven't decided, to be honest. It's a toss-up between a lifetime of torture in a gulag or a firing squad. I'd be lying if I said both didn't possess a certain appeal."

There wasn't much Atticus could respond with so he chose to say nothing. It was all a matter of time now.

Taking a drag of his cigarette, Oliver stared wide-eyed at Atticus. "Are you finally going to admit it?"

"What? That Noel is the most talented of the Gallagher brothers? Yeah, I am. I mean, he wrote all their songs. I know Liam is probably the better singer, but without Noel, Oasis would have been nothing, man."

Oliver stamped his cigarette out in frustration. "I mean that I bettered you. I won. I want to hear you say it."

"That's what all this is about, Oliver? You've been trying to impress me?" Atticus shook his head. "All this, wheedling your way into the KGB, manipulating Shelepin, trying to change history, all of it, was because you wanted me to say how impressed I was? Is that it?"

"No, I mean, no, it's—"

"Because I have to say Oliver, I'm *not* impressed. Not at all. You could have been a force for good, for change, but you chose hollow power, self-interest and a desperate grasp for acceptance. That's nothing to be admired. I tell you what it is, though; it's something to pity."

All colour was stricken from Oliver's complexion, and he looked as though he may throw up. He tumbled from triumph to anguish in a matter of seconds. It was soon replaced by anger.

"No, you are the one who should be pitied, Atticus Wolfe! You!" His fists shook with rage. "You're the pathetic one. You could have joined with me and we could have been invincible. We could have ruled the world, but instead you chose a pathetic existence with a weak woman and an even weaker empire that crumbles by the day. You chose poorly, and for the rest of your miserable existence you'll understand just how wrong you've been."

Instead of rising to Oliver's anger, Atticus inhaled slowly to calm himself. He wiped his bleeding lip on his shoulder. "I tried to help you, Oliver, so many times. I genuinely tried to save you from yourself. But every time, you failed to see the truth. That you're the bad guy, you're the destructive force. The consequences from this point on are all on you. I tried to help you. I'm sorry I failed."

Spluttering indignation, Oliver sprang from his chair and threw his hands in the air. He glanced about, as if searching for someone to gesture to in order to back him up just how wrong a man could be. But there was no one else. Just the two of them.

"Oh, you just wait, Atticus Wolfe, you wait." He paced about, waggling a finger. "I'm going to enjoy seeing you broken down, hearing you finally tell me how right I was all along. It will only make my victory all the sweeter."

Checking his watch, Oliver nodded to himself, as if agreeing with his own thoughts. He knocked on the door.

"I'm not going to wait for some last-minute attempt by your doleful idiot friends to free you. I have a plane waiting to take you now. We'll have the next few months to continue our little chat, believe me."

Visibly annoyed that the door hadn't opened, Oliver knocked again. On receiving no answer, he tried once more.

Eventually movement could be heard on the other side of the door, then the clattering of keys. When the door finally opened, a man stepped in.

"Oh, hey Oliver." The man raised a Beretta M9.

Oliver reeled backwards in shock. Eyes wide in an unbelieving stare, his lips flapped, but nothing audible tumbled out.

"By the look on your face, it's almost like you weren't expecting me?" The newcomer smiled, but there was no humour in Older Atticus's eyes.

SEVENTEEN

"What, what—what the hell's going on here?" Oliver's petrified gaze darted between the two Atticuses. "There's two of you. How can there be two of you?"

"That, as it turns out, is a long story." Older Atticus trained his gun on Oliver. "Arms up. I need to take your gun."

Seemingly too stunned to offer resistance, Oliver relinquished his weapon without a word of protest.

"Sit."

Oliver did as he was ordered. His dumbfounded gaze switched from one Atticus to the other.

Over weeks of observation, Atticus had discovered that his other self's face was far more readable than he'd ever thought. Therefore, by definition, so was his. It was a revelation in some ways, to be able to see himself and read the little nuances and tells he thought were hidden from the world. Right now, Younger Atticus had no trouble reading his other self's emotions. Pure rage pulsed through him.

"You can untie me now." Younger Atticus jangled his manacles for effect.

Older Atticus paced the room, ignoring the request. Either he was too immersed in his thoughts about Oliver, or... Younger Atticus didn't want to complete that thought.

"Atticus..." he began again, trying to get the attention of his older self, but was cut short by Oliver.

"I demand to know how there are two of you."

Older Atticus tapped the butt of his pistol on Oliver's forehead. "You're not in a position to ask for anything."

"But..." Oliver's voice was quieter. It was plain from the confusion on his face that he wasn't coming to terms with the fact that he now had double the nemeses. "How are there *two* of you?"

Younger Atticus sighed. "Remember when I tried to warn you in Moscow? I said I knew how badly Shelepin was going to screw up the world, how he was going to turn it into a nuclear ash heap? You asked where I got the information and I said it was from someone I trusted."

Oliver squinted. "And I said you only trust yourself." He turned to Older Atticus and back again, realisation cascading down his face. "One of you is from... you travelled back in time?" He shook his head. "Ganim did it, didn't he?"

"Too much talk."

Older Atticus grabbed Oliver by the scruff of his neck and yanked him skyward. Either on purpose or due to the sheer shock of recent revelations, Oliver's legs refused to work. He flopped like a ragdoll, unable or unwilling to stand.

"Wait!" Younger Atticus glared at the alternate version of himself. "You agreed we'd talk to him first."

"Before what?" Oliver's alarm visibly increased. "Before you what?"

Younger Atticus had to deescalate this precarious situation. It wasn't Oliver he had to placate. His other self was becoming unhinged. His darting eyes, the clenched fists, the swallowed anger. The man was close to the edge, if not already hurtling over it.

Witnessing the merciless slaughter of his family, the world gone mad, would be enough to push any man to his limits. Younger Atticus also knew that Maggie had rejected his older self's advances. The man had very little to lose, and now he faced the man who had so cold-heartedly put a bullet in the woman he loved. The man could snap at any second.

Younger Atticus tugged at his restraints. "Atticus, untie me. Now."

Instead of moving towards his younger self, Older Atticus shoved Oliver forcibly back onto the hard wooden chair. A compromise that pleased none of them.

"Where... where are the police?" Oliver managed to splutter, regaining the power of speech. "I paid good money for them to—"

"We paid better." There was no humour in Older Atticus's words. "Just the officers, mind you. The others were following orders."

Younger Atticus wheezed, feeling his aching ribs. "Some followed orders just a little too enthusiastically." Perhaps keeping him talking was the best solution. In his compromised position, Younger Atticus had little choice. He leaned forward. "Bribery, in case it was unclear."

Flicking the pistol absentmindedly towards Oliver, Older Atticus said, "Oh, and we know all about Oduwo too."

Never having had much of a poker face, Oliver's lips constricted. "What?"

Uneasily eyeing the pistol dancing in Older Atticus's shaking hands, Younger Atticus spoke up. "We've known for months that Oduwo has been working both sides. He's a double agent, and not a very good one. Our man Cohen spotted it a mile off. Oduwo was just a little too chummy with the local branches. Once Cohen started doing some digging, he noticed reports were strategically missing vital information, which," he shrugged as best he could given his restraints, "and I know you'll find this hard to believe, suited the Soviet Union." He flipped up a hand to dispel a non-existent protest. "I know, I know, but after weeks investigating and laying traps, he fell for each one. The knob. We gave him a plan in its entirety—not the real one, obviously—knowing full well he'd let you know. The traitor did exactly what we expected. Both of them."

For all the danger and agendas floating around the room, Younger Atticus spared a second to revel in Oliver's expression of defeat. "Oduwo is already on his way to Cairo, then back to merry old England. Though I think he'll find it's not as merry as he remembers. England has this weird little quirk where it doesn't take kindly to traitors." He tilted his head. "Isn't that right?"

Oliver offered no reply, not that Younger Atticus expected one. Their multi-layered plan had been executed perfectly. As soon as they'd contacted Cohen directly, he'd told them of his reports on Oduwo. The wheels of MI6 operated slowly, especially in areas deemed less of a priority, so Oduwo remained in his position while London decided how to deal with him. It was Maggie who suggested they use him to their advantage, providing him with their fake plan and knowing it would be too enticing for Oliver to pass up. The cowering man before them was testament to their success.

Danso, the police chief, had promised Oliver if he came alone he'd have ample time with the "captive". He could have Atticus all to himself before he notified the KGB. Instead, Danso was probably somewhere nearby counting his stacks of American dollars.

It appeared not everyone was as enraptured with the plan's success. Eyes locked on Oliver, Older Atticus wiped his mouth with the back of his hand. He raised his Beretta.

"Atticus, we stick to the plan." Younger Atticus shouted, desperate to get through to him.

The door opened and in strode Cohen, oblivious to the commotion taking place. In response, Older Atticus folded his weapon under his arm and greeted the newcomer with a painted-on smile.

"Alright, lads?" Cohen's chipper temperament became muted when he noted the uneasy tension in the room.

Doing his best to lighten the pitch-dark mood, Younger Atticus said, "We were just talking about you."

"Nothing good I hope?"

"Never." Younger Atticus pulled against his handcuffs. "Would you mind?" He glared at Older Atticus.

"Sure, boss."

As Cohen unlocked Younger Atticus's restraints, he jerked his head towards the captive. "So this is him then?"

Rubbing his free wrist, Atticus said, "That's right, you two haven't met."

"Nah," Cohen beamed, "closest we ever came was when he was in a coffin and I shot in his general direction." He lowered his gaze. "But I am disappointed I missed you last time you were in London. You killed good friends of mine when you bombed MI6." He stepped forward, fists clenched. "Though I'm very grateful to meet you now."

"Hold on." Younger Atticus stood for the first time, and

pain tore through his chest. "Everyone," he turned to Older Atticus as he grasped Cohen's shoulder, "calm the fuck down. I feel like I'm herding homicidal cats here. Everyone just fucking chill. We have a plan. Not here."

Older Atticus's gun was out again. "He murdered everyone I loved."

"Not this one. A version of him did."

"I don't fucking care about your fucking semantics. He's a killer. He deserves to die."

"What the hell are you two on about?" Cohen shook his head. "Version of what?"

The bickering seemed to amuse Oliver. Despite the disorder, he'd regained some of his former air of superiority. "Lovers' tiff?" On receiving no reply, his complexion darkened. "What did you mean when you said 'not here'?"

Waiting until he was sure Cohen and Older Atticus weren't going to make a sudden move, Younger Atticus turned to Oliver. "We're going to take you out to the jungle and execute you."

"My country will avenge me, they'll—"

"Not even bother to look." Younger Atticus's stare was even. "You said yourself, the KGB didn't expect any trouble this far away from Europe. Plus, they'll soon find evidence in your hotel room. The easily decrypted notes from MI6 refusing your desperate pleas to come back into the fold. The piles of US dollars. The fake passport. The plane ticket to Madagascar."

Oliver spluttered the start of a response but was cut short.

"You were given countless warnings, Oliver." Younger Atticus's shoulders slumped, for a moment remembering the friend he'd once been. "I tried to get you to stop, but you persisted. This all could have been avoided but you kept at it, even when I told you what would happen. You'll be placed in a shallow grave, far away from anywhere. You'll die alone and forgotten. Nobody is going to build a statue of you. No plaques will commemorate where you lived. Your plans will never come to fruition, your name will be erased from history, on all sides. It's over, Oliver."

Atticus turned to the other two. "We can't do it here, not at the airport. Someone will hear the shot."

"I could strangle him." Cohen mimed for effect.

"But we still have to dispose of the body. We," Younger Atticus glared at his square-jawed counterpart, "stick to what we agreed. It will all be over in an hour. You'll both get your revenge."

"And then what?"

Younger Atticus turned to the older one. He understood what his older self was asking. Once they disposed of Oliver, what was to become of his other self? Did he serve a purpose? Rejected by a version of the woman he loved, where exactly did he fit? While he understood how gut-wrenching it must be for him to see Maggie every day, Younger Atticus had to focus on the here and now. Helping Older Atticus through his immense grief and finding him a place in the world couldn't be done standing there. They would do it, together, but it would have to wait.

Using his handkerchief to wipe the blood from his face, Younger Atticus pointed to Oliver. "We need to get him out of here. Now."

Taking off his jacket, Older Atticus handed it to his younger version. "It'll cover the blood."

They had to act fast; they couldn't be sure when Oliver's absence would be noticed. Oliver had to be in the ground before the KGB realised he was gone.

Police chief Danso had promised he'd provide them

clear passage through the back corridors of the airport and to their waiting car, driven by Maggie. They just had to get there.

Younger Atticus checked his watch. "Where's Danso? He should be here already."

The other two MI6 agents exchanged glances. They didn't know either. For the first time in minutes, a faint glint of hope graced Oliver's face. Atticus couldn't let that hope survive.

"We need to go. Now."

The other two nodded. They'd come too far for it to fall apart now. They manhandled Oliver to the door, then Cohen opened it and peered through the crack. He gave a thumbs up and all four poured into the stark white hallway.

"This way."

Cohen led the way. As they walked, the sound of taxiing planes grew louder. Leaving the building, the sky was pitch black but they were blinded by the bright lights illuminating the single runway. Planes were being loaded with luggage and passengers were ascending stairs. They all seemed oblivious to the intense drama unfolding nearby.

"Help! Help me! I'm being kidnap—"

Oliver's shouts were silenced by a swift jab to the solar plexus. As he doubled over, the other three searched for Danso or, failing that, a way out.

"You there!"

Two men in berets and military green uniforms marched towards them, hands on their Kalashnikovs, their faces grim and determined.

"Help, I'm being kidnapped!"

Swivelling so his back was to the approaching Ghanaian soldiers, Cohen gave Oliver another swift jab, this time lower down. "Stop shouting, you little cunt."

Between wheezes, Oliver asked, "Or what? Or you're going to kill me?" Standing on his tippy toes, Oliver screamed, "Help!"

"What's going on here?"

The first burly soldier kept his hand on his AK-47 but didn't raise it. His partner stood back, both hands on his assault rifle. They were well trained.

"Our friend here is a little drunk so we're taking him home. We don't want to cause any problems, sir."

"This is a restricted area." He jutted his head at Oliver. "Let go of him. Let the man speak for himself."

Given the potential for the situation to spiral out of control, both Older Atticus and Cohen relinquished their grip on Oliver. Instead of pleading his case, Oliver bolted, running blindly into the lights of the runway.

Rocking on his heels, Cohen addressed the soldiers while pointing after Oliver. "Told you. Drunk."

The far soldier stormed forward to join his compatriot. The Atticuses exchanged the briefest of glances. When the second soldier was close enough they simultaneously knocked their AK-47s to the side and landed right hooks, sending both soldiers to the tarmac.

Leaning over the men to ensure they were out cold, Cohen shook his head, impressed. "You can tell you guys are brothers."

Without knowing which way Oliver had gone, they synchronised their watches and sprinted in three directions, agreeing to take him back to Maggie if they found him. They had to cover as much ground as possible before he stumbled upon any more sympathetic ears.

After fifteen minutes of fruitless searching, Younger Atticus came back to the Jeep to find Maggie and Cohen. No Oliver and, surprisingly, no Older Atticus.

Younger Atticus checked his watch. "Where is he? He should have reported back by now."

It was unnervingly like when his older self had disappeared in Siberia. They waited another couple of uncomfortable minutes, each passing second only adding to their growing concern.

Seeing Atticus's mounting tension, Maggie did her best to calm him. "Maybe he's got him and is laying low until it's safe?"

While he appreciated her efforts, Maggie hadn't seen the unhinged glare in the other Atticus. He knew firsthand what an incensed Atticus was capable of.

"Maybe he's just taking longer to look for..." Maggie stood and pointed towards the runway, "Oliver!"

Cohen shook his head. "Yeah, we know who we're looking for."

Smacking the top his head, Maggie pointed again. "No. Oliver. Out there, on the tarmac!"

The two men followed Maggie's finger. Limping, Oliver ran towards a Lisunov prop plane. The markings designated it as an official Soviet government aircraft. It taxied slowly, either getting ready for take-off or having just landed. Oliver managed to reach the door of the Lisunov and yank it open. He was inside before Cohen, Maggie and Atticus could sprint ten metres. They slowed to a halt; there was no way they could catch it. The aircraft taxied towards the end of the runway and then turned as if it was about to take off.

Suddenly Younger Atticus shouted, "The air control tower!"

All three rushed towards the nearby concrete tower. They ascended the stairs three at a time and reached the control room panting. Three men in headsets and crisp white shirts reeled in surprise at the sudden disturbance.

"That plane." Atticus sucked in air as he pointed at the Lisunov. "You have to stop it."

Illuminated by the runway lights, the Lisunov sped down the runway, gathering speed by the second.

"Who the hell are you?"

"I'll explain everything," Atticus said, knowing he could do no such thing, "but you have to stop that plane."

Having reached the end of the runway, the Lisunov climbed into the air, a little unsteady, but climbed nonetheless. Once clear, it continued to rise and turned towards the Atlantic.

"You have to stop it!" Atticus understood how desperate he must have sounded.

"I'll just shoot him down with my missiles, shall I?" the central air traffic control operator offered drolly. "That's a Soviet plane. Do you want me to start a war?"

Atticus's shoulders slumped in defeat. "No, but you will if don't get him back."

The three men in the tower appeared unable or unwilling to respond. Maggie placed her hand on Atticus's arm. Cohen kicked an unoccupied chair in frustration. The air traffic control crew looked on, concerned.

They'd lost Oliver. Again.

Reeling from being so close only to have him slip through their fingers once more, Atticus was already working on what to do next when he was interrupted by a crackling of static from an overhead metal speaker.

"Hello," a voice crackled over the radio, "can you hear me, er, over?"

Flicking a switch on his upright microphone, the central air control operator said, "Say again Victor Charlie one niner? Say again. Please use correct identification protocols."

"Uh, yeah, I don't know what those are."

Cohen, Maggie and Atticus exchanged confused glances. It was unmistakable, Older Atticus was piloting the plane.

Maggie mouthed, *how?*

Younger Atticus shrugged.

His static-filled voice continued. "Can I ask you guys a favour? I need you to pass on a message—"

Atticus hit talk on the microphone. "We're here. We can hear you, Att—"

"My name is Oliver Preston, isn't it?"

Maggie and Younger Atticus blinked at one another. The voice addressing them was certainly not Oliver's. Older Atticus was up to something, but his younger self didn't know the angle just yet. He had no choice but to go along with it.

"Yes it is, Oliver. Just one question, what the hell are you doing?"

"I'm just going to fly out into the Atlantic, far away from the sea lanes, where you can't possibly swim back from, and, well, you know, crash the plane."

The most junior-looking crew member sat up in alarm. "Did he just say he's going to crash the plane?"

"No!" All heads turned to Maggie. Distress smacked across her face, she added, "You can't do that!"

"I assure you, I can. I've wrestled the other part of my self, tied it up and now I'm in control. It needs to happen this way."

The oldest of the air traffic control crew nudged Atticus aside. "Victor Charlie one niner, return to runway one. You have not been cleared for take-off."

"He's right, you can turn around and land." Younger Atticus did his best to remain as professional as he could.

"No. I can't. Remember, I haven't learned the landing bit yet." Older Atticus gave a hollow chuckle. "Plus, if I do, we can't control the situation. No, this is the way it has to be. We're tied together..." he paused as if realising there were other ears listening to their conversation, "...the other part of me. The Soviets, the West. I don't fit in any world."

Younger Atticus understood the last sentence referred to Oliver but equally applied to the man who was actually saying the words.

Older Atticus went on. "It's got to be this way if this is going to end. Oliver Preston has had too many chances, too many escapes. It ends here and now."

"But you'll die." Maggie's voice broke.

"It will be worth it. Plus, there's one too many... of me here already. It has to end this way." There was a pause. "For anyone listening, my name is Oliver Preston. I tried to defect back to England and they wouldn't have me. So I'm forcing this pilot to fly until we crash. It's pitch black out there, you won't find any wreckage before dawn, likely not until well after. There will be no survivors. I'm sorry for all the trouble I've caused."

"Please no!" Maggie was doing her best to keep it together, but all her professional detachment had been scraped away.

Over the tinny speakers, Older Atticus's voice softened. "Before I go, I just wanted to say I love you, Maggie. I know you're not my Maggie, but I love you anyway. Tell that jerk you love to look after you. Believe me, I know how deeply he loves you. He'll make you happy. That, at least, lets me go in peace."

"You don't have to do this!" Younger Atticus gripped the chair in front of him.

"I do." There was a pause as if he were doing something within the plane. "And Atticus? I left you a present in the coat pocket. Make sure you use it."

Static filled the room. All six in the tower exchanged glances, confused for all sorts of reasons. The air traffic control crew over what the hell these strangers were doing and who had just hijacked a plane. Maggie and Atticus over what had happened to Older Atticus. Cohen over all of the above, as well as the sudden affection Robert had for Maggie and now Atticus had for Maggie.

All six stared at the metal speaker.

"Come in. Victor Charlie one niner. Come in."

But there was nothing but static.

CHAPTER
EIGHTEEN

They found the bodies the following day. Flouting among the plane wreckage, the two corpses were bloated and battered by the sea, but it was them. Atticus and Oliver died together.

The official report stated that the dead were Oliver Preston and an "unknown" pilot. The transcript of the air traffic control conversation was handed out to the Soviets and MI6. The Soviets did not press for any further investigation.

In their grief, Atticus's team retraced what must have happened to get Older Atticus on the plane. After Oliver had made a run for it, Maggie, Younger Atticus and Cohen had the airport exits covered. For all Oliver knew, the police were out for him too. His only escape was via one of the planes on the tarmac. Either by observation or deductive reasoning, Older Atticus must have exploited Oliver's desperation. The traitor had sprinted for the only running Soviet plane, like a communist to a manifesto. Unarmed, once Oliver was on board he had no choice but to acquiesce.

Older Atticus's sacrifice appeared to have reset the world.

Brezhnev's visit to Ghana went ahead smoothly. The leaders of both countries were photographed smiling and pointing. The local newspapers stated both leaders promised to forge stronger ties and had many meaningful discussions. It echoed virtually every official visit of a foreign dignitary to another country.

The only distinguishing feature of the visit was that Shelepin left early, and with slightly more protection than would normally have been deemed necessary. It was likely his close ties with Oliver had forever stained his leadership aspirations. Now that his English disciple had been revealed to have been actively attempting to defect back to the West, Shelepin would forever be persona non grata in the upper echelons of the USSR.

Oduwo had been charged and awaited trial. He was being held at Her Majesty's pleasure at Manchester prison, also known as Strangeways. By all accounts the traitor's stay would be uncomfortable and short lived. For the time being, Cohen was running the West African operations until a replacement could be found. He said he'd do his best to not spread chaos across the continent, but couldn't promise anything.

The mission a success, their focus turned inward. The loss of the Older Atticus hit the younger version harder than he could have imagined. For most of their time together, Atticus had been at odds with his counterpart from the future. It was only near the end, when he truly understood the extent of what he'd lost that he began to understand the man himself, even appreciate him.

He had always imagined the two of them would find a workable equilibrium. A way to coexist, somehow. If that didn't work, there was always Ganim's time machine. It was horribly ironic that now Older Atticus had put right the timeline, there could very well be an undisturbed future he could have gone back to. Now he was gone, the loss felt like a gaping wound. Atticus didn't know if it would ever heal.

It hit Maggie hardest of all. She'd taken the death like she'd lost Atticus himself. Which, of course, she had. There were no guides on how to handle the loss of another version of the man she loved.

The grief hung over them like a spectre and followed them all the way back to London. The saving grace was that they had each other to console. They took turns in their grief, looking after each other. It took time, but they somehow managed to restart their lives once more. Together.

Atticus had been on the hunt for Oliver so long he'd almost forgotten how to be a spy without that driving him. Thankfully, he had help. Maggie, of course. Even Rathdowne seemed less aggravated than usual, possibly because now he had half as many Atticuses to deal with.

Atticus had begun a new project recruiting Chinese nationals in anticipation of Mao's Cultural Revolution, which was about to swamp the country. The inimitable Mrs Abernathy was head of the project, and Atticus was happy to be back working with her again.

Irony of ironies, Ganim had been hired at MI6 as a "technical consultant". In fear of him doing something that could wobble the timeline he never actually performed any consultancy, but was paid enough to live comfortably. The fate of his time machine was on the agenda for further discussion, but at the moment they were all so exhausted they were letting it sit for a while. Perhaps one day they'd revisit the matter.

Right now, none of those things were on Atticus's mind. He stamped his feet to ward off the cold. Leaning against a light pole by the Thames in Potters Fields Park, he felt oddly anxious. It wasn't a usual state for him, but here he was. As he thought about it, he realised the foot stamping was more a nervous twitch than an attempt to keep warm.

He saw Maggie approach from Tooley Street, resplendent in her paisley dress, knee-high boots and white trench coat. She was the epitome of the swinging sixties. At first Atticus had struggled to acclimatise to this time; now he couldn't imagine living anywhere else. Or with anyone else, for that matter.

As Maggie skipped towards him, Atticus distractedly fingered the small box in his pocket. For days he'd debated what he should do with the present Older Atticus had bestowed upon him. After all, it was a gift from another Atticus, for another Maggie.

In the end he'd landed on it being a fitting tribute to the two alternate versions of themselves. If those two couldn't find happiness, then it was up to this Atticus and Maggie to find it for them. The ring would be a reminder. They owed a debt to them and would repay it in happiness.

That was, of course, if she said yes. Atticus gulped.

Sidling up to him, Maggie thrust her arms around his chest and kissed him.

"You seem a million miles away."

"I'm really not. I'm," he leaned down to kiss her again, "this far away actually."

She beamed. "I like being this close."

"So do I."

Maggie straightened her back and squinted. "Something's up, you look weird."

"No, it's just my normal face. I always look like this."

Rolling her eyes, she shook her head and dragged him upright. They walked along the path as the sun set over the London skyline.

The scene was vastly different to how Atticus remembered it. From where they strolled, he used to be able to see the Greater London Authority building as well as the Gherkin and Shard office towers. It would be decades before those buildings would even be on the drawing board.

The two strode hand in hand at a leisurely pace, thankful that for at least today, the world didn't rest on their shoulders.

Playfully bumping into Atticus, Maggie said, "So, are you going to tell me what's on your mind?"

Atticus's hand delved into his pocket. "It's more of a question, really."

EPILOGUE

"The bloody wi-fi is down again!"

For effect, Paul Cavendish, MI6 Head Spec Ops, slapped his laptop. It did little to resolve the issue.

On the other side of his desk Eva Destruction and Charles Bishop chuckled, amused at their boss's frustration.

Bishop raised a finger. "Have you tried..."

"Yes, I did that!"

Throwing a sideways glance to her partner, Eva grinned and then turned to her boss. "Paul, you flew in from Geneva this morning. You're not still in flight mode, are you?"

With a frown, Paul pressed a button on his laptop, then turned towards the doorway. "Never mind, I fixed it!"

Eva and Bishop did their best to hide their laughter behind their teacups. Their regular Thursday meetings were a highlight of the week, far less formal than the usual goings on at Vauxhall Cross.

There was a knock on the door. Jarod, Paul's fresh-faced personal assistant, popped his head into the office.

"Excuse me, sir…"

Paul harrumphed. "I said I fixed the thing."

"No, not that. Uh, there's someone in reception to see you."

Checking his laptop, Paul scowled. "I don't have anything in my calendar."

"Yes, I know." Jarod scratched the back of his neck. "The gentleman just walked in off the street, but uh, I think you'll want to speak to him."

"Really, why's that?"

"Because he claims to know what happened to Atticus Wolfe."

All three straightened their backs. The disappearance of tactical officer Atticus Wolfe had stumped MI6 for months. While in pursuit of known terrorist Omar Ganim, he and the suspect had vanished into thin air. No one had been able to get a trace on Ganim, and Wolfe had never returned to headquarters or his home. It was a modern mystery that had completely baffled them all.

"I think you'd better bring him in."

After a few minutes, the elderly gentleman shuffled into the office. Under his arm was a battered canvas satchel. He wasn't exactly frail, though he wasn't exactly sprightly either. Eva, Bishop and Paul made sure the old man was comfortable, gave him a glass of water and then sat beside him in nervous anticipation.

"Perhaps first we could start with your name, mister…?" Paul spoke in his most amicable tone.

The old man chuckled. "That's a far more complicated question than you could possibly imagine."

"Well, see that's the thing, old timer," Bishop stretched, "we're taking time out of our day to hear this news of yours, so I think the least you could do is give us your name.

Makes communication easier, builds trust, that kind of thing."

Unlike the other two, Bishop's approach to the intruder had a far more cynical bent.

The wrinkly old man grinned a yellow-toothed smile. "My name is Omar Ganim."

"Fucknuggets!" Eva stood and planted her fists on her hips. She turned on the old man. "You had me going there, mate. Oh," she shook her hands in frustration, "I thought we'd finally caught a break in finding Atticus."

"Oh, you won't ever find him," Ganim said before smiling again. "At least, not now."

"What does that mean? And who are you, really?" Ganim opened his mouth to respond but Paul held up a hand to stop him. "And don't say Omar Ganim. He's mid-thirties and with all due respect, mister, you're not anywhere near that."

As Paul said the words, he couldn't help but admit there was a certain similarity between the old man before them and the surveillance footage he'd witnessed in the year-long hunt for the terrorist. There *was* something familiar about him.

Bishop leaned forward. "Perhaps you should just say what you came here to say."

"You're going to call me a madman."

"Why's that?" Bishop asked.

Ganim shrugged. "Because what I have to tell you is mad."

Bishop nodded encouragement and motioned for the other two to sit. They did so, albeit reluctantly.

Ganim inhaled, as if summoning his courage. "My name *is* Omar Ganim. I am seventy-nine years old." He paused. "As far as I can work out, anyway. The day Atticus and I vanished was, for me, some forty odd years ago, give or take. You see, the reason you lot were chasing me around the globe wasn't because I was making a bomb like you thought. I was making a time machine." He ignored the sounds of incredulity and forged on. "Atticus cornered me the day we disappeared. Knightsbridge, it was. I detonated the device before it had been properly calibrated, let alone tested. I was flung back to the twenties, Atticus to the sixties. When I caught up with him he was already back working for MI6."

"Wait, what? *What?*" Paul shook his head so much it seemed in danger of falling off. "Atticus went back sixty or so years and worked for us, back then?"

"Look up your records, I'm sure he's in there somewhere." Ganim opened his satchel and handed Paul a thick envelope. "He explains it all in there." He waved his hand towards it. "He slaved over that letter for months, debating what to tell you."

Paul turned the envelope over in his hands, but didn't open it.

"Wait," Eva squinted, "if you met him in the sixties you should be a hundred and something, surely?"

"Ah, well. We built another time machine, you see. Well, rebuilt, really. We had to stop the Soviets from winning the Cold War. That's where it starts to get a bit complicated." Taking advantage of the stunned silence, Ganim said, "You need proof of some description, I imagine?" He pointed at Paul's laptop. "Jump on YouTube." He shook his head and chuckled. "It's been decades since I've used that phrase. Look up the Beatles' last ever gig. The one on the roof of Apple Studios. You all know it."

Too dumbfounded to offer a reasoned argument, Paul

did exactly that. He swivelled the screen around to face the others.

"Find when they start to play 'Don't Let Me Down'. It's when the police show up."

Paul shook his head but did what he was asked. "Honestly, I don't know why I'm humouring you..."

All four watched the screen. It was the familiar scene of the last time the Beatles performed together live. They played effortlessly amongst a smattering of others on the rooftop. Besides the pianist, Billy Preston, there was only one other black face on the roof. Eva, Bishop and Paul leaned in. It took a few separate crowd shots, but eventually they all leaned back.

"My god, it does look like him." Bishop rubbed his eyes.

Paul planted his hands on his hips. "But there's no way we can tell."

As if on cue, the Atticus on screen reached into his pocket and pulled out a piece of white card. On it were two words. He held it up and smiled directly into the camera. The sign said, "Hi Paul."

Eva and Bishop turned to their boss, stunned.

Shaking his head, Paul said, "He could mean Paul McCartney, you know."

The expression of incredulity on everyone's faces soon dispelled that hope. Turning off the clip, Paul turned to Ganim.

"How is that even possible?"

"I have neither the inclination nor the time to go into that."

Face hardening, Paul's eyes narrowed. "If you really are Ganim, I should have you arrested."

Ganim let out a derisive laugh. "Good luck explaining in a court of law why I've aged forty years." He pointed at the envelope. "He explains everything in there. We became friends in the end, if you can believe that. He's a good man, that Atticus Wolfe."

Retrieving a letter opener from his drawer, Paul ripped open the envelope. He skimmed the ten hand-written pages.

"Why didn't he come back with you?" Eva asked.

"He had something to stay for." Ganim grinned as he handed over the satchel.

Paul opened it and pulled out a wad of black and white photographs. "They're... they're wedding photos."

The photos showed Atticus and Maggie on their wedding day, laughing as if they were the happiest people on the planet. There were photos of both the ceremony and the reception. Among the sea of faces were Jimi Hendrix, as well as select members of the Beatles and the Rolling Stones.

"He said he wanted to invite you, but you hadn't been born yet."

Eva pointed at one photo of the bridal party. "Is that the designer Mary Quant?"

Ganim gave her an impressed tilt of his head. "She designed the wedding outfits."

"But what... what..." Paul was at a loss over what to ask.

"That's all I have to say to you good people. Atticus asked me to pass on his message and I've done just that. I hope you have a good life and all, but," he stood with cracking knees, "I'm off."

And there he left them. With their protests echoing in his ears, Ganim strode along the embankment next to the Thames. He was home. It had been forty years, but he was finally back where he'd started. Actually, *when* he'd started. London appeared to be the same as he'd left it, which suggested they hadn't screwed up the timeline too much.

He passed a news stand where a newspaper headline exclaimed, "PM Eddie Izzard in Hot Water". As he crossed over Westminster Bridge, the digital display on Big Ben read ten-thirty.

Ganim frowned. Perhaps their meddling had had some small effect. He wondered what else they'd inadvertently changed. Despite the hiccup, he felt alive once more. For the first time in a long time, he didn't know what was going to happen, and it felt wonderful.

THE END

To be the first to find out when new novels arrive and to win prizes and get free stuff (who doesn't like free stuff?), sign up for my VIP Book Club at:
https://davesinclair.com.au/newsletter/

ACKNOWLEDGMENTS

This book was a total blast to write. By the end I really didn't want to say goodbye to Atticus and his gang, but try as I might I knew the characters not only needed closure, they deserved it. I hope you had as much fun reading the adventures of Atticus Wolfe as I did knocking out the words.

As always the biggest thanks goes to the person I owe for being where I am as a writer – my amazing wife Kristi. Monkey + heart + unicorn. You're everything.

To my extraordinary girls, Quinn and Esther, the biggest hugs for their endless words of encouragement. This book is dedicated to Esther (I'm really not playing favourites, the last was dedicated to Quinn – balance!). Esther, I love that you're writing your own books and forging your own path. You're incredible. Love you so much!

Thanks to the crazy collection of writers known as the G-Mob. These brilliant writers pick me up on the low days and share the highs on the great ones. Thank you for all your support Craig, Justin, Luke, Nathan, Steve, Kat, Amanda and Amanda.

A HUGE shout out to my editor Vanessa Lanaway for her incredible work on this one. Out of all the books I've given her to edit this one was a doozy. What is the correct collective noun for multiples of the same character from different time periods? It still does my head in and I wrote the bloody thing!

Thanks too goes to the very talented Phil Poole who did an amazing job on the covers for the *Atticus Wolfe* series.

Here's a special shout out to Ken Nordli who 'won' a competition via my VIP Book Club newsletter to be murdered horribly (in this book). Well, Ken, you got your wish!

And to my fabulous Book Ninjas who receive an advance copy of my novels – thank you for the never ending positive feedback! You guys rock.

Don't be afraid to reach out on Facebook, Twitter, Instagram. It's always great to hear from readers. You can stalk me at all these semi-reputable places:

www.davesinclair.com.au

https://facebook.com/DaveSinclairAuthor/

https://www.instagram.com/davesinclairauthor/

https://twitter.com/thedavesinclair

https://www.goodreads.com/author/show/ 22167525.Dave_Sinclair

https://www.bookbub.com/authors/dave-sinclair

If you can, please drop a review, it is greatly appreciated. It helps new people discover my work.

Thank you and here's to many more adventures!